SNARLING WOLF

A PIONEER WESTERN ADVENTURE

DAVID FITZ-GERALD

DAVID FITZ-GERALD

Cover design by White Rabbit Arts

Edited by Lindsay Fitzgerald

WELCOME

Welcome back!

Ghosts Along the Oregon Trail was written as if it were a single volume rather than a series of five novels. It has been divided into five books which split the Oregon Trail into segments, or legs, of the journey. Readers will enjoy this series most when read in order, beginning with *A Grave Every Mile*.

Mighty pleased to have you continue on this grueling odyssey.

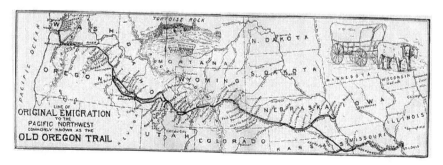

Don't forget, you can find a list of characters online at:

https://www.itsoag.com/gatot-cast.

CONTENTS

MONDAY, JULY 22

I FEEL BETTER THIS morning and I'm glad to be wearing the moccasins Charlotte made. Rose helps me hobble to the privy and balance myself on the rough log as I answer nature's call.

Charlotte offers to sit with me in the wagon, but I tell her I'll be fine today. Then, I suggest she can check on me now and again.

She says, "Alright, dear." Turning toward Rose, Charlotte says, "Let me know if your Mama needs anything." The kindly woman looks at my daughter just a moment longer than necessary, and a tiny muscle in her cheek twitches, ever so slightly. I can't help thinking that my new friend forces herself not to show that she is bothered by Rose's strange appearance.

Arikta passes through camp before our scheduled morning departure. "Fill water kegs," he warns. "Dry camp tonight. Extra half hour before we go." With that, the young scout saunters off to deliver his message to the rest of the emigrants.

When Agapito's horn blows three short blasts repeated three times, we scramble to complete our preparations. The wagons behind us must wait until we take our place in the chain. Instead of helping the children, my incapacity has caused them extra work. I cringe at the thought that the oxen must drag extra cargo today. At least they will only have to bear my weight, and not the additional burden of carrying the doctor's wife as well. I whisper, "Thank you, Hardtack."

The late-July day is hot beneath the canvas. It is to be expected this time of year. Unfortunately, despite the moving wagon and the wide openings fore and aft, nary a breeze moves through the tunnel that feels like a furnace. Oppressive heat aggravates my feverish feeling and I sweat while doing nothing. When I blink off to nap, I'm not aware of having dreamed.

When I awaken, I see Rose's open diary sitting on a box not far from my head. She must have left it there this morning. It's a wonder that the jostling wagon bouncing along the trail hasn't sent the journal careening to the floorboards. Does a young woman her age deserve privacy? Is she entitled to keep her most secret thoughts to herself? Does the fact that she has manic moments change anything? Now that I know about the presence of Snarling Wolf, what could I expect to find out that I don't already know? Rose barely trusts me now. I know I shouldn't read her diary. If she found out, I don't expect that she would ever forgive me. But maybe I could just peek. How would she ever know?

This debate boils in my head all day. Why can't I think of anything else? I almost convince myself that Rose has left her journal open beside me on purpose. Maybe she wants me to read it. Despite the wagon's movements, her notebook stays fully open to a specific page rather than fluttering from one to another. Maybe I'm meant to read just that one sheet of paper. When I finally begin to prop myself on an elbow to see if I can read it from my bed, Rose's face appears in the back of the wagon.

Rose climbs aboard and says, "What are you looking at, Mama?" She scoffs, then picks up her diary and closes it. When she stows it in her satchel, my chance to read her journal has gone by and I'm glad that it will not sit beside me, tempting me, any longer. Rose sits on the box where her secrets were and takes the small mirror from her pocket. Then, she reaches for the black ink and refreshes the obsidian hues on her eyelids. When she's done, Rose glances at me. Her expressionless face doesn't reveal emotion, but the fact that she looked at me represents a small change from the weeks and months gone by. If she was mad about me peeking at her diary minutes ago, she's already forgotten.

When Rose steps from the wagon, I blink off to sleep and begin to dream. I wander through emerald mountain valleys toward a distant peak. The sky grows dark as I continue walking, and in the gloaming, moving spots of light dart recklessly about the gulch. They gather into bright yellow pairs and begin moving more purposefully.

I hear yips and growls as wolf-eyes draw closer and creep toward me as if I cannot see them. Even in the cooler air of evening, my skin feels slippery on the back of my neck. The wolves' jaws snap at my heels and I run madly as if I could outpace them. I'm desperate to escape. I look down at my feet and they're on fire.

As I reach the top of the mountain, I'm screaming, and there's no higher point I can climb to. It is a miracle that I've made it this far without the pack dragging me down.

Just as the wolves' teeth are about to tear the flesh from my bones, I hear the calm voice of a man. He says, "Do not worry, *estimada.*"

The wolves' eyes fade from yellow to bright, like shining diamonds in the black sky.

I struggle to open my eyes beneath the sparkly veil. I gasp when I gaze into the shiny, antelope eyes of the man in my dreams, grateful that he chased the wolves away.

"I am sorry to wake you. You were having a bad dream, no?"

I nod weakly.

"Your little flower is tired and she wants to take a nap. She asked me if she could sleep in the master's wagon because she did not want to disturb you. I told her you would not mind."

I glance at Dahlia Jane and say, "Of course not. I shouldn't sleep the day away anyhow." I hope my smile is reassuring. I thought I was past the delirium and fever, but I can still feel the blood pounding in my veins after another nightmare dominated by the hounds of Hell. "Thank you for bringing Dahlia Jane to me, Agapito."

"It is my pleasure, *estimada*." A long slender finger brushes an errant strand of hair from my forehead. With a final word, "*Adiós*," the man is gone.

When the wagons circle for the evening, I step from the back of the wagon and limp away from camp. After a couple of steps, the gulch I had dreamed about appears before me to the northeast. I hobble forward, putting as little pressure on my bad foot as possible. Andrew, my protective son, appears beside me and points toward the mountain above us. He says, "That's Sulphur Peak, Mama."

I point at the ravine between us and the summit and say, "That's Diamond Gulch, and I'm not going anywhere near it. Have they set up the lady's latrine yet, Andrew?"

On my way to the privy, I hear yowling, but this time it is not a dream. My skin prickles and I wonder whether the foothills of Sulphur Peak are filled with diamonds just beneath the earth's surface and whether wolves lurk within the mountainous shadows.

TUESDAY, JULY 23

I CANNOT ABIDE ANOTHER day of bumping along in the sweltering wagon. Stillman saddles Blizzard for me and the horse dances eagerly, anticipating an adventure. I'm in no condition to gallop across the prairie today. Instead, I sing to calm the stallion. He shall have to be content to walk.

I have missed the company of friends and riding beside them. All that everyone can talk about are the landmarks ahead. The scouts have promised we'll spend the evening at Beer Springs, where bubbly water seeps from the earth, like a sorcerer's fountain. It's hard to believe that such a magical place exists, yet we have seen a drawing of it in the guidebook and read about it in the newspaper back home.

We set up camp quickly at the end of the day, and I wonder whether the children have evaded any important chores. I'll ask about the wagon's axles after we visit the famous springs.

Instead of sending Arikta, Agapito steps into camp. He tells the children, "Bring your cups and sugar." He flashes his dimpled cheeks at me and says, "Don't forget your peppermint and lemon, *estimada. Ándale.*" Rather than share the news with other wagons, Agapito escorts me and the children, leaving Arikta to inform the other travelers.

A magical field of hollow cones stands like an empire of giant anthills. Frothy liquid oozes from the lips of tubular stalagmites, dribbling toward the ground. I watch as Agapito crouches beside a spring that looks like a big puddle. He shows Dahlia Jane how to scoop the foamy water into her cup and then he spoons ground sugar cane into it. He tells her to stir it quickly and then take a sip. "Do you like lemon or mint?"

Dahlia Jane says, "Both."

"Very well. You shall have both, *amorcita*." I limp forward with the small vial of peppermint extract, the larger bottle of lemon syrup, and hand them to Agapito. He adds a few drops of each to Dahlia's cup and says to her, "Try it! *Salud*."

Dahlia Jane repeats his word before taking a sip of sweet, warm soda water, but it sounds like, "Shallood."

Christopher stirs his cup with his good hand, holding the cup awkwardly with the fingers at the end of his broken arm. Because of his sling, he holds the cup close to his body. He must have put too much sugar in his water because it's taking too long to dissolve.

Agapito says to Christopher, "Drink it fast before the bubbles vanish."

Christopher opens his mouth and gulps it down so quickly I wonder how he can taste it. He wipes his mouth with the dirty sleeve of his good arm and frowns. Like me, he isn't one to complain, but the disappointment is visible on his face.

Agapito says, "If you drink it too fast you cannot taste the bubbles on your tongue. Drink fast, but not too fast. Try again, Christopher." Instead of emphasizing the first syllable of his name as most of us do, Agapito emphasizes the toe sound in the middle. It sounds to me like, "Crease, *toe*, fair," only the r rolls off his tongue at the end.

Instead of flavoring his soda with lemon *and* mint, Christopher chugs a cup of one and then the other. He says, "I like the mint better," and wipes the suds from his face again.

Agapito says, "I like the lemon better." Andrew agrees with Agapito.

Instead of adding extract or syrup to her cup, Rose stirs her soda water with a sprig of sage.

Agapito says to Rose, "I never thought of that and I have never seen anybody try it. Is it good?"

Rose nods before she takes a sip and then again afterward. It is almost as if she decided to like it before she took a taste.

We sit and watch other travelers taste the enchanted water. It feels like we are a large happy family and I'm glad that Agapito and Stillman are here with us. Agapito stretches his thin legs on the gentle hill beside me as we relax in the shade. It is as if we're enjoying a Sunday afternoon picnic. He says, "How do you like The Oregon Trail Oasis, *estimada*? Many people claim that this is their favorite stop."

I turn my head and smile. I say, "It is nice, Agapito, but not as nice as Scotts Bluff."

He grins back at me and says that he must agree. Then, he guides us 200 yards along a path that leads to a musical geyser. Every fifteen seconds, the solid rock whistles like a steamboat and jettisons a fountain of water from a hole maybe a foot wide. Agapito says, "This is Steamboat Springs."

Clouds gather and afternoon showers interrupt our break. On the way back to camp, Agapito offers me his muscular arm. I grab hold of it and daydream about marrying the cheerful Mexican, despite the foolishness of such a notion. He bends slightly at the waist, looks into my eyes, and holds his gaze for a few seconds before we stroll and my heart races.

The cloudburst drenches and soaks us before we make it back to camp. Feeling childish, I imagine skipping through the rain, arm in arm, and laughing.

The Viper can't stand being separated from his brothers, yet he frequently needs time alone. Usually sitting alone on the porch while his brothers play cards in the cabin satisfies his need for solitude.

After years of promising a luxurious retirement, The Viper regrets creating an expectation of leaving the remote camp on Birch Creek. How can he walk away from his favorite place in the world? Why should he have to?

Whenever the Viper and his brothers seize an emigrant's wagon, they haul the stolen rig to their compound and park it in a ring beyond the cabin and corrals where they keep the stolen stock. The Viper's brothers know not to disturb their moody sibling when he wanders among the decommissioned rigs. Like tombstones in a graveyard, the retired wagons stand, frozen in time, all that remains of each family's dreams. Dreams that never came true.

His favorite wagon has a sign that reads, 'Clayton Stonecipher and Sons.' The Viper struggles to remember the day he and his brothers captured the Stonecipher family's wagon, or what the man, his wife, and sons looked like. The outlaw speaks to the patriarch as if they were friends, and Clay were still alive.

Oftentimes, The Viper sits on the back of Clay's wagon, swinging his feet and staring off to the west. Why should they have to quit? The Viper doesn't want to move to the coast and frolic with prostitutes like his brothers do. He doesn't want to sit in a saloon and play cards. They don't belong in places with lots of people. This is where The Viper thinks they were meant to be. He tells the ghosts that he needs to stay and watch over their things. Should I let my brothers go without me? Can I hold them here as prisoners? Maybe I should kill them. What if they tell somebody about this place? We can't have that, can we? Why do things have to change? Can't they stay as they are now? It's getting harder and harder to keep this family together.

The Viper cocks his head as if listening for a response. What ghost would answer such questions?

As if giving it more serious consideration, The Viper spits out words that only ghosts could hear. "I couldn't kill my brothers, even if I wanted to. Could I?" *Even if he could kill Sloan, what about Leon? What about The Radish? Would he rather die himself than kill his youngest brother? What if he just abandoned them after delivering them to the coastal city of their dreams? Then, he could be alone all of the time. A wistful pang flashes through his chest. As much as he likes to be alone, could he live that way forever? It crosses his mind that he needs his brothers more than his brothers need him.*

WEDNESDAY, JULY 24

LATE IN THE MORNING, we reach another fork in the path. One trail is known as Hudspeth's Cutoff and leads to the California gold mines. From this point forward, our path will be less crowded. I remember thinking that it would be nice to have fewer wagons on the trail. I had looked forward to separating from the would-be miners. Now, the idea of traveling a less populated path seems terrifying. As they say, there is safety in numbers.

We pause for an early dinner beside the sparkly water of the Portneuf River. After our repast, we tiptoe a few hundred yards along the bright beck and peer at Sheep Rock. We were warned to approach the hillside silently, and we are justly rewarded.

A stalwart, Rocky Mountain sheep watches us from a rocky outcropping. The ram's thick horns curl on either side of his head. When we step across an imaginary line, the bighorn nimbly twists, clacks his hooves across the rocky crag, and crashes into the branches of a wide tree.

A disappointed sigh passes through my windpipe. It's too bad we couldn't have gotten closer, but we were lucky to see the majestic animal.

When we return to the wagons, our fellow travelers are ready to continue the day's journey. We turn north and follow the lonely trail that leads away from the gold mines of California. Like Larkin dreamed of doing, so many travelers plan to turn south along Hudspeth's Cutoff, and I wonder if we'll have The Oregon Trail to ourselves.

When we reach the thin trickle, our guides call Tenmile Creek, I watch my children tend to the late afternoon chores and then disperse. They used to spend so much time together, but now it seems they can't wait to go in different directions at the end of the day.

Rose takes an empty flour sack from the back of the wagon and moves from one sagebrush to another. I limp along, keeping my distance from her, and notice that she only cuts the branches on the west side of each shrub. When I catch up to her, I chance to ask a question and hope that she will not have an emotional outburst. "Why do you only cut a few branches on one side?"

She says, "West represents the setting sun and the darkness at the end of the day, just like the paint on my eyelids. It also represents death, Mama."

I gasp when my daughter speaks of death, like the difference between life and death is plain as night versus day. Larkin said to leave her to work her fears out on her own, but now, she seems to welcome such conversation. I say, "Would you like to talk about that, honey?"

Rose says, "Mama, I see dead people." She looks at me and then she looks to the west. "That's what I do. I see 'em. They talk to me. And, I help them if I can."

I don't know what to say. I feel my lips fluttering, but words don't come to mind. Of all the things Rose could have said to me, this is the last thing I expected. Knowing that Indians think she is a shaman hasn't prepared me to hear these words. What's strangest of all is that she doesn't sound angry, like she usually does. Her words and sentences suddenly sound mature.

Rose's normally blank face twists in what looks like an uncomfortable expression, and she continues. "People look blurry to me, but when I see ghosts, they are clear as crystal."

How is it possible? I had no idea that Rose had difficulty seeing. I say, "Why haven't you ever told me that before?"

Rose turns her head, looks at me, and lifts her lip in a full sneer.

I guess I blurted my query. I should have held my tongue or spoken more softly. I add, "We could have gotten you spectacles."

Rose ignores my words. "I have a special guardian angel, named Janey. She's a beautiful Indian with long black hair. She helps me when I feel lost and asks me many questions. Her questions help me to see what I should do."

I'm stunned. I don't know what to say or do. My eyes dart to the left and right of Rose, as if I expect to see her imaginary friend, though I know there's no such thing as ghosts. Then, as delicately as I can, I say, "Is she here now?"

"No, Mama. It's just us. I didn't want to tell anybody, but she thinks you should know."

"About the ghosts?"

Rose frowns at me. "Um. Er. Yeah. Not just about the ghosts." Rose turns away from me. She sniffles and then says, "It was an accident, Mama. I didn't mean to kill him." She stops, takes several short breathes, and mangles a sprig of sage within her tightly clenched fist.

My hands find my face. I'm shocked by what Rose is saying. I blurt, "Him? Who? What? You killed a man?" It isn't like my daughter to jest. I add, "When?"

Rose speaks so quietly that I must follow her as she continually turns away from me. It's hard to hear what she says. Her voice sounds wispy, like a tendril of smoke. She says, "I just wanted to scare the man and make him leave. I was afraid of what would happen if he didn't go away. I took Pa's gun and I followed him. It was so dark." Rose pauses for a moment, touches her right palm with the tip of her left index finger, dropping the crushed sage, and then continues. "The gun got heavy and my hand was sweaty. My toe tripped on a rock, the gun went off, and the man went down. Then, I ran away. I didn't know what to do." She begins to cry before she finishes speaking and sobs into her hands.

I try to comfort Rose. I tell her not to worry. I walk around her and pull her close. After a year of turning away from me, Rose clings to me. Her revelation unleashes a floodgate of repressed emotions and I do my best to console her. I tell myself that my daughter is not a murderer. I say to Rose, "There, there, honey. It was an accident. A terrible, awful tragedy, but everything will be alright now, Rose."

I close my eyes and rub her back. I can't believe my daughter killed a man. All this time, I worried that Larkin had killed Bartholomieux. Every time I hold the Colt Walker, I get a sinking feeling that the bullet that killed the lecher came from Larkin's gun. It turns out I was right about the revolver, but only briefly did I ever think about the possibility that Rose had squeezed the trigger.

Rose's tears begin to subside and I continue to reassure her. "You don't have to worry about Bartholomieux anymore."

Rose's sobs return with a vengeance. I try to hush her, then say, "What's wrong, honey?"

"You don't understand, Mama. It will *not* be alright. It will *never* be alright again. Bartholomieux is angry. He wants revenge. He is even more wicked than we imagined and his spirit is powerful. His ghost takes possession of the bodies of living snakes. He likes to commandeer the biggest ones he can find, and when somebody kills that snake, his ghost leaves before the snake dies. Bartholomieux delights in the act of slithering. The sensation of rubbing himself along surfaces delights him. He says the most awful things to me, Mama."

"Good Heavens, Rose. I've never heard of such a thing. You must be imagining things." I don't know what else to say to my daughter.

"I knew you wouldn't understand, Mama. That's why I didn't want to tell you. When it comes to spirits, you're such a dolt." The harsh words come with a spray of saliva and I realize that I'm standing too close to her. She looks at me and sniffles some more. "A dorbug has more of a sense of *spirit* than you do."

Dorbugs are crusty beetles that feast on dung. "Why must you insult me, honey?"

Again, Rose ignores my question. She says, "Even a buffalo gnat is more perceptive than you."

I say, "Goodness gracious, honey. That's not very nice." I shouldn't feel insulted. Rose is right. I have always had trouble fully believing in God, or the Devil. The idea of ghosts has always seemed utterly ridiculous to me. "I must insist that you speak to me with respect, Rose. Now, try to put these foolish notions aside."

Rose says, "It's alright, Mama. Mehitable told me that most people don't understand." She turns away from me again as if she considers our conversation finished.

"Mehitable?" In my head, I picture the lovely, older woman. When I was Rose's age, I was obsessed with Mehitable's son, Noah. I always expected that Mehitable would become my mother-in-law. She is strange, and hard to get to know, but also kind and sweet. After knowing her my whole life, I'm sure that if the woman claimed to see ghosts, I would know about it.

"Yes, Mama. Mehitable helped me understand ghosts and not to be afraid of them. I wish she had come with us."

I can't help feeling exasperated. "Good Heavens, Rose. Is this what troubles you, child? I had no idea."

"I know, Mama. Nobody knows. Nobody except for Snarling Wolf, Sees Through Clouds, Janey, and Mehitable." She sounds at peace, and then she juts her chin forward and says, "Don't you ever call me 'child' again, Mama."

"Very well, honey." I turn away from Rose's rebuke. Her mention of the man who wants to marry my daughter makes me shiver. I keep reminding myself to accept it. I can't help but stutter. "I don't know what else to say. It's a lot to hear all at once." I'm sure that the shock and guilt that comes from accidentally killing a man has caused all this ghostly nonsense. I don't have the heart to tell her that I think she's gone mad. She doesn't need to hear that. What she needs now is compassion, so I say, "What shall we do?"

"I don't know yet, Mama. Just be careful of rattlesnakes. I don't know if the demon wants to kill you, me, or all of us."

The creepy feeling of an invisible serpent slithering around my neck makes me shake violently. I steel my nerves and try to dispel the thought. My daughter expects me to believe that a ghost inhabits the bodies of snakes. It's the most ridiculous notion I have ever heard, but she seems genuinely concerned. I can't deny that our snake encounters have been fearsome and they seem to be getting worse. Since Rose has confided in me, I wonder what will happen if I go along with her. I ask, "Are you sure there's nothing we can do? How do we make him go away?"

"I don't know, Mama. I have some ideas. I'm hoping my guardian angel will help me. She doesn't like to talk about it. I don't want to talk about it anymore either, Mama. Not tonight, anyway."

I ask Rose about Snarling Wolf. She says that she doesn't expect to see him for a few days and I wonder where the man went. I feel guilty for hoping that he will fail to return, but can hardly help myself.

THURSDAY, JULY 25

Do I BELIEVE THAT Rose killed Bartholomieux? It's a hard truth to accept. It's heartbreaking, as a parent, to think that my child has killed somebody, but it isn't like she killed the man in cold blood. She only meant to send the man away. Everybody in town wanted that horrible man gone. Why on earth did my daughter think that *she* should be the one to face him? I can't believe I fantasized about a dalliance with the cad. What did Rose call him? A demon! Good Heavens.

Do I believe what Rose said about ghosts? How did she know that I don't believe in spirits? Does what she said change my mind at all? If it were true, it *would* explain a lot. One thing is sure, Rose believes. Perhaps it is enough that I know *that*. How ironic? Larkin thought that she had an unhealthy preoccupation with death. If he only knew what was *really* going on. What if we had tried to talk to her? Would she have told us then? I should never have let Larkin convince me to leave Rose alone. She needed us and we failed to help her.

Since Rose's revelation, I've noticed long strings of twisted sage have appeared like gigantic necklaces around the necks of our oxen and the horses. Perhaps she believes that sage protects us from evil spirits. The kine don't seem to mind, but Christopher rolls his eyes and twirls a finger near his temple when he looks at the oxen. It's the first time I've noticed the other children inferring that Rose is going mad. Mostly, they have been content to ignore and overlook her strange behavior, but have their feelings changed now? Have they discussed the matter between them, or is Christopher's gesture a fleeting moment?

When we anchor our prairie schooner along Twentyfour Mile Creek, I hobble to the wagon and remove our blankets. With several vigorous snaps, I dislodge all the dust I can shake from our bedding and wish that I could take a proper bath in the trough of a brook.

After supper, Rose joins me as we visit with friends. While I hold Jenny and talk with Cobb, I can't help noticing that Rose is distracted. She stares at the side of the Banyon's wagon, and nods subtly. I touch her shoulder and she says, "Yes, Mama," but she doesn't look away from the wagon. "What do you want?"

Instead of trying to explain Rose's behavior to Cobb, I pass the baby back to him, asking if he needs anything. I don't know how he manages to care for the baby as well as Bess, Joe, and the oxen, not to mention the tiny apple trees, but he does. He's an example of what people can accomplish when there's no choice to make but to face each day head on.

We spend a few minutes visiting our friends in each of the next couple of wagons before ambling back to our own. When we pass the Banyons' again, Rose's gaze transfixes on the wagon side as before. In a hushed voice, I ask her, "What do you see, honey?"

Rose flashes a glance at me then returns her attention to Cobb's wagon. In a husky voice that doesn't sound like Rose, she says, "It's Jennie. She wears a brilliant white dress and sits with her legs crossed on top of the provision box. She watches Cobb and the children. Sometimes, she reads stories from a heavy book that seems to float, untouched, in the air before her. I try to tell Jennie that she can watch over her family from Heaven, but she refuses to vacate. She doesn't argue but quietly insists that she will follow and stay with them until Cobb's apple trees bear fruit in Oregon. She says her family needs her. How long will that take, Mama? How long will it take before the seedlings are full grown? When will they bear fruit?"

What do I know about orchards? I try to recall whether I know anything about the subject, and then hazard a guess. "It might be five or six years, I think."

Rose says, "That's too long. She should cross over."

What is Rose talking about? "What do you mean, cross over?"

She shrugs and says, "Oh, Mama. Don't you know anything? She needs to make her way to Heaven. It's not good for a spirit to stay here too long. This is not where spirits belong. It's not good for the soul, and it's not good for the living."

I try to imagine that I can see a ghost in the dusky shadows of Cobb's wagon bonnet, and I can feel my cheeks tighten. I shake my head and say, "I'm doing my best, dear, but it is difficult to believe such things are possible."

Rose turns abruptly toward me. Through pinched lips, she spits, "I knew you wouldn't understand." Then she pivots and storms away in the opposite direction from our wagon. I turn and follow her with my eyes until she darts between wagons and disappears. I feel like I've been very understanding. What could have upset her so? Perhaps it is time to discipline her like a child, if that's how she chooses to behave. I don't mind her having preposterous fantasies, but she must learn to treat people politely. We've never tolerated rudeness in our children until this past year, and I think it's about time to try a different approach.

I take a few more steps toward our wagon and gasp at the sight of Galusha and his shadow, Samuel. They're crouched behind Gwibunzi. The mare is still tied to the wagon. I hasten my pace and direct my steps toward them. I shout, "Get away from there."

Perhaps the men were spying on me, though I can't imagine why. Samuel bolts into the shadows, but before Galusha can get away, the startled mare pulls her hind leg forward toward her stomach and boots her hoof into Galusha's head, sending the scoundrel flying.

FRIDAY, JULY 26

I'VE BEEN IN A foul mood all day. After spending half the night helping Hollis and Charlotte doctor the miscreant, Galusha gained consciousness and demanded we fetch Mortimer Meadows. When Hollis brought the groggy preacher, Galusha said, "That woman's wild horse tried to kill me and I want it destroyed." Then, Galusha conveniently loses consciousness, though I suspect he faked it. Captain Meadows glowered at me, told me we'd discuss it later, and muttered the word misfits as he turned back toward his wagon.

During the day, I drove Galusha's oxen, despite my bum leg, while Pamela tended her husband in their wagon. Their children, Henry and Maggie, marched along, like silent soldiers. When we reached our destination at Cabin Creek, I was neither thanked for helping them nor condemned for Galusha's incapacity.

It's not my fault that the nitwit crouched behind a horse. Everyone knows better. Even children understand that they should not put themselves in such danger. The wretch has done nothing but goad me, and yet I step forward to help his family, despite my lame leg. I shall not make the same mistake again tomorrow. Let someone else play good Samaritan.

After supper, I saddle Blizzard and ride off alone. I rein the stallion toward a mountainous ridge to the southwest and glance back at the wagon train. Arikta follows on Howl a comfortable distance behind me. I should feel guilty for causing extra work for the dutiful scout, but I need to escape the rolling village for at least an hour or two. Let him follow if he must.

I squeeze my legs together before swinging my head forward and Blizzard lurches from a trot to a lope. Moments later, we pass the rising ridge to the right and run haphazardly into a man's camp. Blizzard skids to a stop beside a campfire, throwing a cloud of dust at the man who doesn't seem at all startled.

For a moment, I'm stunned. My slow-moving brain seems to have failed me. Finding another person in this desolate country is so unexpected. Then I realize that the man is an Indian. It dawns on me that I've met this man before. With a gulp, I recognize the Brulé shaman. Snarling Wolf effortlessly stands and holds his hand forward in greeting.

As I slide from Blizzard's back, a tempest of thoughts swirls in my head. What should I say to this man? All I can think of is the fact that he is closer to my age than Rose's. It has been a week since I learned that Snarling Wolf followed the wagons.

I feel disarmed when he offers me a cup of coffee. Instead of a tin cup, he hands me a hollow buffalo horn. I thank him, and he acknowledges, "*Tó,* you are welcome, Mrs. Moon."

"Good Heavens. You remember my name?"

"Yes, of course. Do you remember my name?"

"I do." The image of Rose sitting on the Indian's lap a week ago flashes in my mind.

"I thought you had forgotten."

"No, I could not possibly forget you, sir."

A strange expression appears on the Indian's face. "I have never been called *that* before." He crosses his arms over his bare chest.

"Goodness gracious, I'm sorry, Snarling Wolf." I struggle to avoid making a sour expression, but I loathe speaking his name out loud. Perhaps he could teach me how to say his name in the Lakota language.

I jump when Snarling Wolf calls out to Arikta, who has failed to sneak up on us. The Pawnee scout leads his horse into the Lakota shaman's camp. Snarling Wolf makes the hand sign for *friend* and says, "This far from home, we are not enemies." I had forgotten the animosity between the Pawnee and Lakota people.

I introduce Arikta, and Snarling Wolf introduces himself to the scout. It sounds to me like, Song Manitu Tanka Glow. It is a lengthy name, but the first three parts run together quickly. I try to repeat the Lakota name. It feels better not saying the English words, though the meaning is the same. I'm sure there is a reason for the moniker, but if there's a story, I'd rather not hear it.

I ask, "How does Rose know when you are near, or where to find you? She gets lost so easily."

"The same way I know where she is. Our love finds a way. We have been together for many lifetimes, Mrs. Moon."

If I could see my face, I'm sure it would reflect the doubt I feel inside. I struggle to maintain my composure. Has the whole world gone mad? Am I the only one that thinks the idea of specters is absurd?

The Brulé tells us that he has been hunting and asks if we are hungry. I answer that we have just had supper and he motions for us to sit beside his small fire. Once seated, cross-legged on the ground, Snarling Wolf looks at me, hands resting on his knees, and an uncomfortable silence envelops us.

My heart races and I search for something to say to the man. I fill the empty air with a question that I've been pondering. "What's the difference between a shaman and a medicine man?"

Snarling Wolf leans slightly forward and gently nods. "A medicine man is a healer. A shaman is connected to the world of spirits. Both have great power."

"What is the world of spirits?"

"The echoes of our ancestors that live with the Great Spirit."

He doesn't seem to have more to say about the matter. I rub my chin and wonder what he means by echoes. I understand that Indians refer to God as the Great Spirit. "So you are like a preacher? A man of God."

"Yes. It is so."

"How old are you, Song Manitu Tanka Glow?"

He seems pleased to hear me attempt to say his Lakota name. "I have counted thirty winters, Mrs. Moon."

"Good Heavens." I would have guessed the handsome man was half a decade younger than that. "I am only a few years older than you are." Without thinking, I continue. "Perhaps you should marry me instead of Rose." My right hand finds my cheek, and I'm surprised by my own words. I notice Arikta edging away from the firepit.

Snarling Wolf looks into my eyes and gently says, "Yes. Perhaps I should, but that is not what the Great Spirit intends."

"Dearie me. You think that God wants you to marry Rose?"

"It is so. I gave my word. I promised I would wait until she is a woman. Then, when she is in love with me, we shall marry."

"I know that Indian women marry young, but I would like Rose to wait."

"How long?"

"Four years? Maybe two? She only just recently turned thirteen years old."

"Mrs. Moon, Rose is no longer a girl. She is a woman already."

I cannot argue the point. Rose's menses have commenced, and despite her slender form and loose-fitting clothes, she has matured physically, if not completely. Though I wonder how Snarling Wolf knows this, I'd rather not inquire. "I don't think she is ready. Couldn't you come back in a couple of years?"

Snarling Wolf grunts. "No. We already have a deal, Mrs. Moon. We will not wait."

SATURDAY, JULY 27

ASIDE FROM THE MAN'S name, prominent incisors, the way he wrinkles his nose like a wolf about to bite, and the fact that he wants to marry my daughter too soon, I can't help but like the Brulé shaman. I imagine the Indian trailing the wagon train, perhaps a mile behind us as we trudge along Camp Creek. All those times I felt like somebody was watching me, hunting us, preparing for an attack. All along, it was Snarling Wolf, shadowing our excursion. I ruminate on ways to delay what is probably inevitable. Song Manitu Tanka Glow. The man's name reverberates in my mind as I turn it repeatedly on my tongue.

After dinner, we depart the little creek we have been following, finally reaching a feeble waterway called Ross Fork at a place between tall, treeless mountains. Beyond our temporary habitation, the trail leads through the narrows we will penetrate after two nights at Ross Fork. A sojourn here would be welcome if the grass were more plentiful.

When everyone has settled into camp, The Committee makes an unwelcome appearance beside our hearth. First, Captain Meadows tells us about Galusha's unimproved condition. "It will take the hunter a long time to recover from his head wound." As usual, I'm distracted by the movement of Captain Meadows' nose as it careens about on his flat face. Even so, I can't help hearing the threat as he says, "I've said it before, that misfit Hellhorse is a danger to us all. It doesn't belong in a civilized encampment, Mrs. Moon. I think you should return the mustang to the wilderness."

I can't help but defend Gwibunzi. "But Captain Meadows, Gwibunzi is not a Hellhorse. Galusha and Samuel surprised her with their sudden movements. They should have had more sense than to squat behind a horse, and don't forget the time they set off firecrackers beneath Gwibunzi's feet. I'm sure the horse has not forgotten them. Horses are very smart animals, Captain Meadows."

The captain flashes a quick frown. "I had forgotten about the firecrackers. Even so, a wild animal can never be fully tamed. I don't want to see that horse in camp. She can stay on the picket line, or you may hobble her. I don't mind if she stays with the cattle, but I don't want to see her tied to your wagon. Do you understand?"

It hardly seems fair, but at least he isn't demanding that I turn the mare loose. His words are not hard to interpret. I say, "Very well, Captain Meadows." For a long minute, he lingers, pursed lips pinched tightly, and moving slightly. Is the man contemplating more serious punishment for Gwibunzi? Is he thinking about whether to add another subject to our discussion?

The rest of The Committee and their wives stand crowded together behind Captain Meadows except for Dottie Crouse, who wanders through our camp and looks into the faces of my family around our firepit. She's like a sergeant inspecting an army of soldiers.

Dottie says, "What about that girl, Mortimer. Have you seen the Devil's paintbrush has touched her eyelids? And what of those heathen adornments? It isn't right." The tittering woman bends her arm and places a hand on her hip, waiting for the captain's decision.

"No, I see what you mean, Mrs. Crouse. It isn't right, is it? Would you do something about the girl, Mrs. Moon? What's her name again?"

"Her name is Rose." I glance at my daughter and I can see flames of anger in her eyes. I tell him, "I shall think about it."

The captain returns his attention to the matter of Gwibunzi. "I still think the best thing to do would be to banish that misfit nag. See that she stays out of camp, Mrs. Moon."

When The Committee is gone, Rose stands, passes her half-eaten supper to Andrew, and walks along the estuary to the southwest. After a couple of minutes, I follow her.

The meandering trickle of a creek is barely visible beneath thick scrubby shrubs. Snarling Wolf's camp is at the base of a steep hill and his small fire's smoke is diffused by the branches of a tortured tree with twisted branches.

I say, "Good evening, Song Manitu Tanka Glow." He tips his head forward, slightly, acknowledging our arrival.

Rose says, "What are you doing here, Mama? Why have you followed me?"

With my head forward, I stubbornly say, "I just wanted to tell you that I have no intention of asking you to discard your jewelry. I will not ask you to stop wearing the black paint. I only told Captain Meadows that I would think about it so that he would go away. He was more interested in banishing Gwibunzi anyway."

Snarling Wolf says the mustang's name and I realize that he's asking a question. "Gwibunzi?"

"Yes, we call the three colored mustang, Gwibunzi. I believe it means scorpion in Shoshone."

"She is a powerful horse."

"Thank you. Would you like to ride her?" The way he says powerful makes me think he's suggesting the horse isn't just an impressive physical specimen. His tone has an ethereal sound, as if Gwibunzi were a magical creature rather than a common, potentially outlaw, wild mustang.

He nods.

"I'm glad." The other reason I followed Rose is to ask a question. After a quiet moment, I say, "If you and Rose marry, would you make your home with us in Oregon?"

Snarling Wolf frowns and shakes his head. "No, the Brulé need us, Mrs. Moon. We shall live as Lakota."

My hands join at my stomach and I look down at my tightly intertwined fingers. I say, "I see. I'd rather you reside in Oregon for a couple of years first, and then if you want to return to the plains, I will understand."

The shaman says, "We shall see, Mrs. Moon."

Rose looks at me like she'd rather I were thousands of miles away. I turn and make my way back to Ross Fork. It's going to be a challenge to keep my family together.

SUNDAY, JULY 28

WHILE WASHING CLOTHES BESIDE the river, I notice a lone rider on a cremello. The light-colored horse reminds me of Rio, Agapito's golden mare, only this horse has frosty white socks, tail, and mane. The slouching rider looks downtrodden.

I abandon my pink dress on the washboard and rub my wet hands on my chocolate-colored apron as I stand. I say, "Hello, stranger. I'm Dorcas Moon. You look hungry."

The plain looking young man motions toward his head as if bringing his hand near the brim is good enough to imply a tip of the hat. He must be exhausted. He says, "Name's Larry, ma'am. Larry Pritchard."

I inquire, "Where are you going, Larry?"

"Back." He nods almost imperceptibly toward the east. "Home. To Missouri, ma'am. My brother got kilt and I had enough of the west."

With a frown, I think about yet another story of death. "I'm sorry about your brother, Larry. Get down and let me feed you something."

Larry grabs his saddle horn with both hands, swings his right leg over the cremello's rump, and falls in a heap on the ground beside his horse. I hurry to the man's side and help him to his feet. With one hand at his waist and the other on his shoulder, I realize that there is no meat on this man's bones. "When was the last time you had something to eat, Larry?"

"Don't rightly remember, ma'am."

Larry's horse follows as I guide Larry into camp. Fortunately, the horse looks much better than his master. I help Larry sit beside the fire and pour him a cup of coffee. The appearance of a stranger among us begins to draw a crowd. I set a skillet on rocks at the edge of the flames and begin frying the last of our bacon.

Agapito steps from the master's wagon and introduces himself to Larry while Andrew scribbles notes in his journal, no doubt he's excited about writing a feature story about the starving stranger. As I return from the wagon with a couple of biscuits, I hear Agapito say, "Tell us your story, if you would, *Señor*."

The man already appears a little livelier. A spray of crumbs spews from his lips as he laughs at Agapito's question. He gestures toward the cremello. "My horse is named *Señor*. Perhaps he can tell you a story."

"That is a nice horse, *hombre*."

"Thanks." The edges of Larry's mouth sag in a melancholy frown. "He's all I got left."

Agapito says, "It sounds like you have seen *el elefante*, no?"

I have heard countless downtrodden people speak about the high cost of experience as having seen the elephant. The Spanish word sounds very similar to English.

The thin man's chest heaves as he takes a deep breath, as if he intends on telling his whole story in one big sentence. "Me and my brother Charlie started for Oregon without a wagon. Along the way, we met up with others traveling alone, camping out under the stars along the way. There were eight of us at Alkali Springs, a day beyond the Malheur River. Charlie rode ahead to scout, and he never came back. Neither did his horse. We heard gunshots. I jumped on *Señor* and dreaded what I might find. In the distance, I saw three riders and four horses galloping northward. The robbers scalped Charlie to make it look like Indians got him, but they were not Indians. Then they turned Charlie's pockets inside out and rode off with his horse, *Señorita*. We weren't just brothers, we were also best friends. The cross-country adventure was his dream, but I couldn't let him go alone. Now, I can't go on without him. All I can think of is having to tell Ma that her youngest son is gone."

Rose sits beside the fire, her gaunt body twisted away from the crowd. She stares at the ground beneath our wagon and mutters unintelligibly, like someone chattering in their sleep. Her utterances are very quiet, but don't go altogether unnoticed.

The nervous crowd of gathered emigrants question Larry relentlessly, but he has nothing new to add. Instead, he patiently answers them without revealing additional information. Aside from describing the thieves as *not* Indians, Larry offers no further descriptive detail.

I jostle the sizzling bacon in the skillet and then stir batter for pancakes. The young man's sad story brings tears to my eyes and I think about another casualty of the unmerciful Trail. I try to remember the locations he has mentioned, Alkali Springs and Malheur River. How many rivers, marshes, ponds, and springs have we encountered that could have borne such names?

With his hearty meal finished, Larry Pritchard grips the horn and drags his malnourished body up into his saddle. I try to convince him to spend the night and have a couple more meals with us, but he says that he won't rest until he returns home and delivers his devastating news. The last words he says to us are, "We loved riding matching horses, me and Charlie."

When he's gone, our friends and neighbors disperse. Dahlia Jane plays with Bess and Joe at the Banyon's wagon, and the boys have wandered away. Rose still sits beside the fire, looking distracted, like she's trying to focus on the movement of insects, but her attention keeps returning to the space beneath our wagon.

Finally, I sit down beside Rose, and say, "What's wrong, honey?"

She says, "It's Carter. He doesn't want Stillman to be alone."

I guess she would have me believe that she has been speaking with Carter Wilson's ghost. I thought they only came out at night, but that's not the point. I say, "Stillman isn't alone, dear. We are his family now."

Rose says, "That's not what he is talking about." Stillman appears from behind the wagon carrying my pink dress, washboard, and bucket. Rose finishes by saying, "Carter wants Stillman to find somebody else." Stillman drops his burden, turns, and walks away. He must have heard Rose.

MONDAY, JULY 29

IN THE MORNING, I'M relieved when I see Stillman, but the sentiment doesn't last. He tends to the usual chores, but he moves away whenever I approach. Yesterday, I worried when he vanished. Before bed, I finally found him standing night watch, and when I waved, he turned his back to me.

I don't know how much Stillman overheard of my conversation with Rose. If he had heard the whole discussion, he would know I didn't tell her about his relationship with his fake cousin. It's just like the time Rose called Esther's baby, Armand. Esther *still* thinks I violated her trust and now Stillman must think I've revealed *his* secret. I told him I wouldn't say anything. I haven't uttered a word about it. When I get the chance, I'll let him know.

At least my bum leg has healed. Today is the hottest day yet. As we pass through the narrows of Ross Fork, the vast valley beyond blurs in the haze. Though I'm no longer lame, I saddle Blizzard, preferring to ride rather than walk. Andrew passes Dahlia Jane up to me and we spend most of the day on horseback, talking about her fantasy world inhabited by feline-faced humans.

I can hardly believe it has been a month since we left Fort Bridger. The sight of Fort Hall appears like a mirage and I think of the many natural wonders we have witnessed since we left our mountainside home last year. After a long time in the wilderness, there's something comforting about the sight of a man-made structure. From a distance, I don't know whether the walls are made of stone, wood, or mud, but it appears as if someone has painted the fortification white. Perhaps it's coated in the same bleached dust that clings to us.

The joyful shouts of fellow travelers are accompanied by triumphant blasts of Agapito's bugle as we announce our arrival to the fort's inhabitants. We make a hasty encampment on the banks of a wide river beyond the palisade and everyone is eager to explore. Agapito steps into our camp and I ask him about the waterway. He says, "It is the Snake River, at long last, *estimada*."

I tremble at the introduction. As much hardship as the other rivers have wrought, fear of the notorious Snake seems to choke my windpipe. My trepidation must be apparent. Agapito says, "Try not to worry."

"How long must we endure the presence of the Snake?"

Agapito lifts an eyebrow and I can tell he would rather not answer my question. "Perhaps six weeks."

"Good Heavens. That seems like forever."

"I wish I had better news. Will you visit the fort today?"

"Yes, I'd like to. We don't have a lot of money left, but I hope to find bacon, flour, and coffee."

Most of the other travelers have already departed. Dahlia Jane tugs at my dress and Agapito asks if he can escort us. I tell them to wait while I get the small purse of coins from the wagon. I feel the flutter of anticipation in my belly as we approach the gate. I've never been jealous of women who live in cities or big towns, but I must admit I'm excited to taste a morsel of civilization again.

The first thing I see when we pass through the gates is Christopher. The boys went ahead, and Christopher says he has seen everything. He's short of breath and as he pants, he asks, "Where's Pa's watch, Mama?"

"What do you want that for?"

"There's a man here who can fix anything." With his good arm, he grabs my hand and drags me to a donkey cart parked in the middle of the parade ground. "This is my friend, Tinker Potts, Mama." That boy makes friends quickly.

The bald man wears a hat that's too small for his skull. He's a strange-looking fellow with the bushiest eyebrows I ever saw and a pointy beard perched on the tip of his barbed chin. Gleaming jade eyes glance at Agapito then back at me. "Howdy ma'am. Burton Potts at your service. Understand you got a broken pocket watch. I can fix it." He gestures behind him and I see a hoard of ticking clocks, pocket watches, gears, and assorted scraps of metal.

Christopher runs off to fetch the timepiece. While he's gone, I examine Mr. Potts' impressive collection.

When Christopher returns, clutching Larkin's watch, he pants, "Can you fix it, Mr. Potts?"

The tinker makes ticking noises with his teeth as if imitating the sound of passing time. He flips the watch in his hand, winds it, and pops it open. "I can fix it for a dollar, ma'am. Do you know how to wind it?"

Christopher says, "Yes, Mr. Potts. We sure do."

"You don't *overwind* it, do you?"

My son says, "No sir." I don't know how Christopher would know. Larkin never let anyone touch the timepiece.

The tinker chatters while he works. "You headed to Oregon?" When I confirm that we are, he continues. "Careful ahead, ma'am. It seems that this year, there are twice as many murders and robberies as last year, and last year was a bad 'un." He laughs as if he finds such atrocities amusing.

I gasp. "Good Heavens."

"Yes, ma'am. Why, yesterday, a woman carrying a baby told me that she was forced to watch as a pair of bandits staked her husband, spread-eagled between two trees and shot him full of arrows as if he were a target to practice on. Then, they scalped him. I guess they want people to blame the Indians."

Mr. Potts puts his lips on a small tube and blows air through the gears of Larkin's watch. Then, he continues his story. "Good thing the lady's husband was a drunkard, because she escaped on an old mare when the highwaymen passed out. Guess they liked the man's likker." Tinker Potts lets out a howl and says, "Then again, if he weren't a sot, maybe their wagon master wouldn't have banished them from their wagon train. Poor lady. Cute baby girl, though."

My fingers shake as I pay the tinker. It is hard to justify spending a dollar on the repair when we have so little money left, but how could I tell Christopher no?

TUESDAY, JULY 30

IN THE MORNING, NOBODY can find Stillman. Addie Bull says she saw Stillman buy a mule from a woman who sells marmot skins and vegetables at the Fort. Garland Knox says he saw a man riding south on a mule in the twilight last night. I rub my eyes with my palms and think, *I've got to get him back.*

At the wagon master's hearth, I plead with Agapito. "What can we do? How can we find him?"

"What if he does not want to be found? What if we find him and he does not want to come back?"

"I guess I'll be forced to accept it, Agapito. He's old enough to be on his own. I know that, but something is telling me not to let him go."

"He has not been the same since he lost his..." Agapito taps his chin, pauses, and says the word in Spanish, "*primo.*" He looks at me nervously and says, "I did not want to say anything, *estimada*. Do you know about Stillman?"

I grip the Mexican's shoulders, look left and right to make sure that nobody is listening and say, "Good Heavens, Agapito. Whatever do you mean?"

"One night—it was the day we crossed the Wakarusa River, and Carter lost his hat. The evening you found the dead body. The one that the wolves dug up. Do you remember, Dorcas?"

I tip my head forward and nod, wishing that Agapito wouldn't remind me of wolves, and hope that he'll hurry up and get to the point.

"I saw a silhouette of Stillman and Carter in their wagon. Sometimes light reveals the shape of things behind a canvas. There is no mistaking what I saw, *estimada*. The cousins were more than *amigos*. I have met men like them before, and I do not care about such things, but The Committee must never know about Stillman."

I let go of his shoulders and grasp my head in my hands. "They were not cousins, Agapito. Nobody knows but me. And you, I hope. Only, somehow, Rose knows something too. Stillman overheard Rose talking to me about Carter. He must think I told her his secret. Now he's gone. We must get him back. Can you help me find him?"

"No, it is not for us to do." Agapito's clenched lips shift back and forth and his eyes cast about. I wonder if he's trying to think of what to *do* or what to *say*. Finally, he says, "I think I can send Dembi Koofai. It is a good thing that we spend a second day at the Fort. Dembi Koofai is the best tracker and this is still Shoshone country. Can you write a letter for him to carry? If Stillman does not want to come back, at least you can let him know how you feel."

I throw my arms around Agapito and his body relaxes within my embrace. His strong arms circle my back and he says, "Try not to worry, *estimada*." I am comforted, but still worry.

After carefully counting our remaining money, I return to the fort with a quarter, and Rose joins me. I want to talk with the woman who outfitted Stillman with a mule and it wouldn't hurt to buy fresh vegetables.

The middle-aged woman lives in a small cabin just outside of the fort. She sits on a small porch scraping a pelt and stands when we approach. She has triangular-shaped eyes, pinched lips, and a small mouth. She nods her head and says, "Be with you in a moment, ma'am."

After quickly dipping her hands in a bucket of water, she dries her hands on her apron and introduces herself. "Name's Abigail Trudgeon, but please, call me Gail." Her mouth is so small that I can't help staring at her lips when she talks. How does a woman with a mouth so small keep from starving?

After introducing Rose and myself, I ask her if she could tell me about the young man who purchased her mule. She scratches her hip and says, "Handsome young man, mighty polite too. But he seemed distracted. Paid me thirty dollars. Didn't even dicker."

"Did he say where he was going or why?"

"Naw, not that I can recall. What's it to ya anyway?"

"He's been traveling with us since last year and we've grown fond of him. He's kind of like a son to me and I hate to see him run off."

Rose stares at an empty stool beside Gail's chair and her face twitches as if she's listening to an imaginary conversation. She doesn't seem to hear us.

Gail says, "Men ain't good at staying put, if you ask me. I got used to it a long time ago. Every spring my Henry gets an itch to go somewhere and promises to return with sacks o' gold. Cain't count on that, nope. That's why I sell veg'ables and varmints."

Her greens are wilted, the peas are shriveled, and most of her green beans look like they've got lichens growing on them, but her robust carrots make my mouth water. She says they'll keep all the way to Oregon. Then she shows me a pile of yellow-bellied marmot skins. "Stitch enough of 'em together and you can make a warm blanket or coat."

I can't help imagining the woman with a mouthful of peas firing them from between her lips at the yellow-bellied marmots, and start to giggle. "How do you catch the rodents?"

"I trap 'em. It's easy and they're tasty." Her tongue darts out, moistens her lip, and retreats into her mouth, like a frog snatching a fly.

She says, "Goin' ta Oregon, ain't ya?" I nod, and she shakes her head. "Road gets dang'rous ahead. People been robbed and kilt. Don't see why you don't just make this yer home. Neighbors is friendly and that shack is abandoned."

I thank the woman and tell her that we have our hearts set on Oregon. I purchase five pounds of carrots, a pound of withered peas, and a marmot skin.

Gail says, "That'll be twenty-five cents."

I bargain her down to twenty cents, hand her the coin in my pocket, and tell her to keep the change. She tilts her head, wags her finger, and says, "I like you, yes I do." Her cheeks rise, and her pinched lips push away from her face in an unusual, closed mouth smile. It occurs to me that she resembles the rodent that feeds her.

On the way back to camp, Rose tells me Henry was bludgeoned by outlaws with his own pickaxe and buried beneath the entrance to his mine. She says, "He sits on the stool beside her and he told me that she would wring his neck if she knew that he got his self kilt."

Good Heavens, what an imagination that girl has.

The Viper's heartbeat quickens. "Sloan, where's The Radish?"

"Why? Who cares?" The man shrugs and says, "I think he said something about riding up Hog Creek to look for gold in that old man's cave. You said we could take the rest of the day off."

"I changed my mind. We've got work to do tonight. Confound it. That idiot ain't never gonna find no stinking gold." The Viper considers sending Sloan to fetch The Radish but worries that The Radish might not obey conveyed orders. He crushes his hat tightly onto his head and says, "I'll fetch the kid."

It's a long ride and many miles between the cabin and Trudgeon's mine. The Viper curses under his breath. What was he thinking, telling his brothers they could take time off in the middle of the summer.

Horse and rider have both worked up a sweat by the time The Viper reaches the mine on Dead Indian Mountain. The Viper hears the taps of The Radish's pickax as he chips away at the walls of the cave.

Inside, The Radish has built a small fire. He is shirtless, but chalky dust sticks to his sweaty skin, and in the dim light, he looks fully clothed.

Impatiently, The Viper asks, "Find anything?"

The Radish seems pleased with his brother's question. "Naw, not yet."

The Viper would rather yell at the youth or whip him for wandering off without permission. He must constantly remind himself that his brothers aren't enemies. Though he couldn't care less about their hopes and dreams, he must at least pretend, or he might lose them, or have to kill them. "We gotta get back. The pilgrims are hoping we'll take their horses tonight. There's a handsome looking string of nags on a poorly placed picket line."

The Radish asks for ten more minutes and his wish is granted.

The Viper tells him that he'll wait outside. Walking away, The Viper ad-monishes himself. If you're nice to people, they take advantage of you. That's true whether those people are strangers or brothers. *As he crosses the threshold, he hacks a wad of phlegm and spits it on the ground, just above where Henry Trudgeon's bones are buried.*

WEDNESDAY, JULY 31

I'M DISAPPOINTED AT THE first light of day. After wandering off yesterday afternoon, Rose has not returned and now, I'm forced to pray that she has spent the night with Snarling Wolf. The alternatives are far worse. What's more, Dembi Koofai has not come back. I had hoped to find Stillman sleeping beneath the wagon, this morning, but he is not there.

Boss Wheel is furious about our extended sojourn at Fort Hall and he is not alone. Captain Meadows' nose dances around his face as he protests our delayed departure, though he is the one that always insists we refrain from traveling on Sundays. Others echo Captain Meadows' complaints. As usual, Agapito tries to point out the bright side, if you could call it that. "The mules and oxen need more time to graze."

I can't remember Boss Wheel criticizing Agapito in front of a crowd before. Today, he says, "You should not have sent the Shoshone after that greenhorn. If the fool doesn't have enough sense, by now, to stay with the wagon train, who needs him?"

When Rose disappeared at the Big Sandy River a month ago, the wagons continued forth and we caught up with them at the Green River. Despite

Boss Wheel's harsh criticism of Agapito, I'm grateful that the ramrod isn't willing to leave without his scout, now that we've reached the sinister Snake River.

I worry endlessly about the health of our oxen. The Devons have done a tremendous job of dragging us through the wilderness. Today, while they rest, I decide to work for *them*. Andrew and Christopher join me, though Christopher isn't much help with his arm still in a sling. We labor with the sickle all day, yet only manage to drag seven sheaves back to our wagon. That's less than half of what we cut back at Red Buttes. The grassy meadow nearby could hardly be called abundant.

Our bellies growl at us for having skipped dinner, but the boys do not complain. I think of poor Larry Pritchard, going without food for so long, and then I think of Cian and Oona Reid, surviving famine in Ireland. Missing a meal to feed our stock hardly seems like a hardship worth mentioning.

When we return from cutting grass, I prepare supper in silence. Then, I leave Dahlia Jane with Andrew and walk away to the south. I watch the horizon, praying to see the black Appaloosa and the flop-eared mule carrying the Shoshone scout and our lost companion.

While wishing preoccupies my mind, I yearn for Rose's return. Not just from the arms of the man with whom she spent last night, but also from the strange thoughts that trouble her mind. I try to convince myself that prayer would serve me better than self-pity and make a rare request of the Lord.

There's nowhere elevated to perch, so I sit cross-legged on the level ground. I glance to the right and watch the bright orange sun edge toward the distant horizon.

When I look back to the south, I see a solitary rider approaching. It's surprising to see how near the horse appears to be since I looked in that direction moments ago. I think I would have noticed the emergence of a dot on the skyline.

Seeing anyone in the vast wilderness is unusual. Perhaps the horseman is a trapper, like Lucky Nye. I suppose the rider could be Dembi Koofai, returning alone, but that would mean the worst has happened. I can feel my spirits sinking as I begin to grieve. It's hard not to worry. What if something terrible has happened to Stillman? Maybe he has succeeded in evading the scout's search. If only I had a spyglass, like Boss Wheel. Then I'd know. The world seems to be full of *if onlys*. If only this. If only that. Good Heavens.

Another rider gallops past me and I jump to my feet. Clipper's thundering hooves pound the ground and Boss Wheel's baggy capote flutters in the wind as he rides toward the approaching horse. I squint and realize the approaching horse carries two riders. A slouching body rides fore and the tall scout sits aft.

I resist the urge to run toward the riders and suspense builds within me as I bounce on the balls of my feet. Is that Stillman riding in front of Dembi Koofai? What about the mule that Stillman purchased from Gail Trudgeon? Two men riding one horse is never a good sign.

The sun has disappeared over the edge of the world by the time they reach me and I'm frantic with worry. Dembi Koofai stops briefly beside me. He says, "He's hurt," leaving the 't' off hurt as he always does.

Stillman moans, but at least he's conscious. Dembi Koofai reaches around Stillman, stretches his arm toward me, and passes my letter to me. Dembi

Koofai says, "Found him jus' wes' of Rattlesnake Peak. Mountain lion raked his back. Firs', I found his half-eaten mule."

My hand claps over my mouth. An image of a cougar devouring a mule comes to mind. I can almost feel the claws tearing the skin on my back as I picture the cat's attack on Stillman. My eyes blink furiously and the mountain lion becomes a pack of wolves in my imagination. "Oh, Dembi Koofai. Thank Heavens. What would have happened if you hadn't found Stillman?" Of course, I know the answer to that question. There's no way Stillman could have survived. If the mountain lion didn't return to devour him, the buzzards or wolves would have left his bones to bleach in the relentless summer sun.

Boss Wheel says, "Talk later." He groans as he twists in the saddle and I can hear his joints crack as he straightens his body. "Let's get back to camp."

I glance at Stillman and then, look back at the wagon master, and ask, "Will he be alright?"

"Don't know." His shoulders jut forward and then back. "I seen men die from less. Not up to me."

Thursday, August 1

Last night, Hollis and Charlotte doctored Stillman's back and the patient spent the night in our wagon with the fresh cut hay. Dahlia Jane and I crowded into the tent with the boys.

Soon, the wagon train will leave without us. Rose is still not back. Her disappearance is not a mystery. I know who she's with even if I don't know where they are.

After three nights at Fort Hall, the rolling village must return to the wilderness. I dread telling Agapito and Boss Wheel, but I can put it off no longer. The ramrod is behind schedule. Normally, he's in the saddle before the rest of us rise. At least the wagon master and his assistant are together and I'll only have to say it once. I cross my arms and look at the ground between them and say, "Rose didn't come home last night."

Boss Wheel says, "I know."

I look at him and his stern face neither encourages nor discourages me to say more.

"She didn't come home the night before last either."

Again, the chief guide says, "I know."

I close my eyes and feel my body tense. "The Brulé shaman has been following us. I thought he would forget about Rose, or I would never have let him think that he could marry her someday. I know that Rose is with him, only I don't know where they're camped."

"I do." The former mountain man points to the north and I see Rose approaching. She carries a bag with her, the one that she filled with sprigs of sage a week ago.

"Dearie me, Mr. Roulette. I was afraid we'd have to remain behind this morning."

"That girl's gone wild. You had your chance to tame her. Now, it's too late. Get used to it, lady."

I'm surprised by the master's harsh words. Instead of arguing with him, I run toward Rose. Hot, angry tears quickly give way to a sense of relief. When I reach Rose, she looks at me like I'm a curiosity. It is as if she returned after an absence of fifteen minutes rather than two days. She says, "What's the matter with you, Mama?"

"I was worried about you, honey."

She speaks to me as if telling me about an everyday matter rather than a life changing event. "You will have to accept Snarling Wolf, because I am his woman now, Mama. We were married in the river the night before last."

"Oh, honey."

"Why do you sound sad? Can't you be happy for us? Pa is."

She doesn't say much but always says the most preposterous things. She's going to need to grow up fast now. "Rose, darling. Your father died months ago."

She looks at me with a frown. "Mama, I told you, dead people speak to me. Pa left us for a while when we abandoned his safe, but now, he's back."

Nine blasts from Agapito's trumpet interrupt our reunion. Losing Larkin was horrible, grieving was painful, but we have had to march on. I'm not willing to accept the thought that somehow, as Rose suggests, he has returned to watch over us as a ghost.

Rose says, "Snarling Wolf has gone hunting. I'll walk with you today."

I sigh, relieved to know where she is. I have so much I want to say to Rose, but there isn't time. The wagons have begun to roll and we run to meet our moving wagon. Andrew and his one-armed brother have completed the morning's chores. Christopher greets us cheerfully from his place beside Hardtack, bullwhip in his good hand.

Rose falls in beside Andrew as I climb into the moving wagon. There's barely room for me, and the smell of fresh hay stirs when I sit upon the sheaves. Stillman lies face down on my narrow bed. He props himself on his elbows and frowns at me, like he wishes I weren't here. The angry red gash on his exposed back extends from the top of his right shoulder to the small of his shiny back. Charlotte must have applied some sort of poultice to his scar.

My heart melts when he looks into my eyes. Stillman blinks rapidly as he looks over his shoulder at me. He says, "He saved my life, Dorcas. Dembi Koofai saved my life."

I think back to when Stillman had cholera. I feared that it would take him like it did Larkin, Ellen, and Carter. Now, we almost lost him again. Words don't do my emotions justice. My voice cracks when I say, "I'm glad, honey. Why did you leave us? I was so worried."

He says weakly, "I heard you talking to Rose."

"And you think I told her about Carter?"

"Yes. You promised you wouldn't."

"I didn't, but somehow she knows."

Stillman groans.

I say, "Nobody talks to Rose or listens to her for that matter, if it makes you feel better, Stillman." He lowers himself back onto the quilt that covers my bed plank. I run a motherly hand through his hair and he listens as I tell him about Snarling Wolf and Rose. Saying the words out loud is painful, but somehow therapeutic.

Stillman says, "She can't help who she loves. I don't think we choose; love chooses us."

"Oh, Stillman. It isn't who she loves that bothers me. She's so young, that's all. And I wish that the man had a different name, but I'll get over that." After a long silence, I wonder whether Stillman has fallen asleep. I whisper, "Promise me you'll never leave again without saying goodbye. I know you're a grown man with your own life to lead, but losing you and Rose feels the same, Stillman. I couldn't love you more if you were my own son."

Stillman moans again and mumbles, "Yes, ma'am. What will you tell everyone about me now?"

I pat his left shoulder. "I will tell them the truth. You set out to seek your fortunes alone, but a catamount decided it wasn't yet time for you to be on your own. How's that?"

His muffled voice says, "I should have known better than to doubt your word, Dorcas."

I rise to leave and say, "I know. Try to get some rest, dear."

FRIDAY, AUGUST 2

I DON'T CARE WHAT Captain Meadows or The Committee thinks of me and my family. Our fellow travelers will have to accept us, or not, as they wish. If the friends who accompanied us on this expedition now judge us unfit company, so be it. If our new friends want to ostracize us, we shall have to endure the separation.

If it weren't for Rose's age and her troubled mind, I'd be delighted that she has found a man that she loves. I never knew that it would be so difficult for me, but now I know that it isn't easy to surrender a child to adulthood. I tried to put Rose off and I realize there's nothing I can do to halt them. I could no sooner stop the wind from blowing, the rain from falling, or the sun from shining.

After a second day of traveling along the serpentine river, I need to distance myself from the confines of our traveling village. Instead of saddling Blizzard, I amble lazily away from the circled wagons, southeasterly, in the opposite direction of the river.

The diligent scouts who are so keen on following me when I ride away from camp have failed to notice my escape on foot. A mile from camp, the soil turns from fertile to barren. I sit on an inviting boulder near short, red-tinged mountains and stare absent-mindedly at the horizon.

The empty wasteland has come alive. A lizard scrambles across a nearby rock. The longer I sit, still as a stone, the more active the panorama becomes. I'm surrounded by a city of marmots, warily watching out for one another. Many feed on the vegetation while others stand erect, perched on their hindquarters.

As I watch the busy rodents, I think of the woman at Fort Hall, and the many different names she used to describe them, including rock chucks, ground squirrels, and whistle pigs. Gail must have found a similar field for her deadfalls.

I recall the prairie dog I pegged with Larkin's rifle near Courthouse Rock. That was May, now it's August. So much time has passed by, and so many things have happened.

I should shoot the chubby animals. Fresh meat is always welcome in camp, but I have no desire to hunt today. I yawn and shift my position. The nearby sentries sound their alarm. Their shrill whistles almost sound like screams and it is unnerving when several sound off at once.

Again, I sit still and the whistle pigs begin to chatter rather than scream. They grunt and squeak at each other as if they are having a conversation. I watch a pair of amorous pups play patty cake with their tiny paws, then rub their noses together. I can't help thinking of Violet and PBJ while observing the affectionate creatures.

When a wide-winged raptor soars overhead, the frolicking varmints scramble to safety. After the danger has passed, their wiggling noses peek from their burrows. Ten minutes later, they seem to have forgotten that they live in a dangerous world. Is it the same with our rolling village? After each tragedy, a couple of days go by, and we distance ourselves from the latest horror. Before long, we've put one hazard after another behind us, accepting that hardship is not extraordinary.

After another fifteen minutes, I see a massive, slow-moving, yellow snake that could be as long as I am tall if he were stretched taut. Somehow, the wary rock chucks fail to notice the wretch, slithering along the base of a large rock. I'm tempted to jump to my feet or climb on the rock and scream, but instead I feel like I'm caught in a trance, hopelessly watching the inevitable tragedy unfolding before me.

The tiny pups, barely larger than chipmunks, play like children beneath parked wagons. The yellow reptile inches toward the infant marmots. I should jump to my feet, flail my arms, and warn the creatures of the danger.

I cringe as the viper strikes and admonish myself for not saving the tiny rodent when I had the chance. I remember wondering why nobody did anything to help Pamela when Galusha beat her. When Bobby and Wayne begin tossing their fists at each other, why doesn't anybody else intervene? I should have warned the unsuspecting rock chucks and deprived the Devil's spawn a meal. Instead, I sat by and watched; nature took its course.

In the wake of the snake's attack, the chattering marmots scamper to the safety of their burrows. I doubt their underground dens offer much protection from rattlers looking for squirming whelps. The juvenile rodent is a substantial meal, even for the flaxen viper and instead of retreating, I watch for a while as the snake ingests its prey.

When I return to camp at dusk, I kiss the children goodnight. Stillman has left his sickbed and Charlotte thinks he should leave his shirt off so the air can heal his wound. Fortunately, the long scratch across his back is shallow. Stillman is lucky that the catamount was hungry for a taste of old mule rather than a belly full of human flesh.

After wishing everyone a good night, I step toward the picket line. Once again, it is my turn to stand watch and I remind myself that I insisted on sharing this burden.

At midnight, when my shift is over, I shimmy into bed. I'm surprised that my youngest child has fallen asleep alone and I'm careful not to wake her. Stillman has returned to his usual place beneath the wagon. Having missed bedtime, I imagine Stillman telling Dahlia Jane stories from beneath the wagon or singing her lullabies until she fell asleep. I seek sleep, but it is slow to come. I can't stop my worried tears, nor can I overlook the fact that Rose has not returned from her evening visit with Snarling Wolf. I remind myself that she has told me that they are married now.

My family will never be the same.

SATURDAY, AUGUST 3

THE BEAUTY OF AMERICAN Falls overwhelms me. Crashing water thunders over a steep precipice. The roaring sound of cascading water reminds me of the dangerous river's evil intentions, yet my eyes enjoy the feast.

Our view of the cataract from a high bank slightly to the south includes three ghostly, hunched-over buttes in the hazy background. The torrents crash a hundred feet and it looks as if the water boils. A prominent island, with basalt boulders and tall pines splits the waterfall at its midpoint, extending from the top of the falls to the bottom. Tall rocky spires poke up from beneath the rushing water like giant marmot statues, perched on their haunches.

When Rose departs from camp, I follow her, leaving the evening chores to the boys, yet again. She turns her back to me and ambles toward the grazing cattle. She sets her bag on the ground and pulls out a long strand of sage. When she finds Hardtack, she strings the artemisia over his neck, and ties the ends together. Who ever heard of making necklaces for cows? I watch in amazement as she similarly adorns all our oxen. Then she pulls a handful of sage from the bag and rubs her hands together as if lathering her hands with soap. I don't suppose she's harming anyone with her strange obsession with the pungent shrubbery.

When Rose is finished with the sage, she strolls toward the river. When she steps onto a narrow trail that looks like it leads down the steep banks, I wonder where the path leads. I imagine animals use this narrow footpath more than people do.

When Rose reaches the water's edge, she jogs to Snarling Wolf's side. The Lakota's spear has impaled a thrashing salmon. It looks like the mortally wounded fish still expects to escape into the river as the Indian sets the spear down and encircles Rose within his long arms. I haven't thought about how I should behave as a mother-in-law. I clear my throat as loudly as I can, hoping that they hear me over the sound of the falls.

Rose frowns at me as I say, "Good evening, Song Manitu Tanka Glow. Rose tells me you are married now."

"Yes. It is so. She said she loves me. We made our promises to each other and we have bonded."

I repeat the word as a question. "Bonded?" Then I realize what the man means and add, "Oh, I see."

Snarling Wolf says, "For now, I will share her with you."

"So you will travel with us to Oregon?"

"I don't know how far we will go. I don't know how long we will stay. It is for the Great Spirit to decide. For now, we will follow the thunder wagons. We shall see."

"I understand that you and my daughter have made promises to each other. Will you make me a promise also?"

"What is your wish?"

"Do not leave without telling me. If you must go, let me know. I couldn't bear it if you disappear with my daughter, and I don't know you've gone."

"I understand. I promise. We will not leave without telling you."

I might say more to the man if Rose weren't standing beside him. What will he do when she looks at him the way she looks at me? Will she shoot daggers at him with her glances once the newness of her love for him wears off? Perhaps a mother-in-law must learn quickly what to say and what not to say. I inhale and ask, "Will you be camping here beside the river?"

"No. We will stay just above."

As I make my way back up the herd path, I recall having just invited the Indian and my daughter to join us for supper tomorrow. I was so distracted and relieved to know they wouldn't mysteriously disappear that I don't remember the man's response to my invitation. I decide that I will ice a wedding cake, regardless. Perhaps it will help me accept that Rose is a new bride.

When I return to camp, Charlotte is looking at Stillman's back from inches away. Andrew blows the ink dry on today's issue of *The Times*, and Christopher pokes at the embers of the fire with a stick.

I sit beside the boys and Charlotte also takes a seat. As she grinds powder in a bowl, I think of Rose turning charcoal into black paint.

Dembi Koofai stands midway between our camp and the wagon master's. His long hair hangs beside his cheek, yet he watches us from the corner of his eye. I wave him over and he turns to see whether my gesture is intended for someone else.

As the scout slowly paces toward us, Stillman's torso twists awkwardly, like a contortionist. He says, "my back itches something fierce."

Dembi Koofai speaks to Stillman, "Never knew an' one survived a puma before."

Stillman looks up at the Shoshone and says, "Thanks to you. I don't know what would have come of me if you hadn't shown up when you did."

Charlotte passes a small clay bowl to Dembi Koofai. "You saved his life, now help me heal him."

Dembi Koofai kneels behind Stillman, dips his index finger into the unguent, and gently traces the scar. Stillman appears to shiver as the slippery balm covers his gash, and Charlotte commences to grinding another batch of medicinal ointment.

When Charlotte finishes, she hands the bowl to me and says, "For tomorrow" and returns to her wagon. Dembi Koofai fades into the shadows as darkness quickly follows dusk. Dahlia Jane lies sleeping at my feet, curled up like a kitten, and the yawning boys retreat to the tent.

For a while, Stillman and I sit silently together beside the fire. Stillman interrupts the tranquility. "Dembi Koofai said you wrote me a letter."

"I did." I remove the tattered paper from the deep pocket of my dress and hold it up for him to see.

"Can I have it?"

"It doesn't say anything more than I've already told you, Stillman."

"That's alright. But I'd like to have it anyhow. Nobody ever wrote me a letter before."

SUNDAY, AUGUST 4

AT BREAKFAST, ANDREW ASKS, "Did you read *The Rolling Home Times,* Mama?"

I stop stirring the batter for tonight's cake and look up at him. I can't remember the last time I read the paper. Why does the thought of reading Rose's forbidden journal seem tantalizing, whereas the publicly posted news of the day seldom draws me to the center of the ring? I'm proud of Andrew's commitment to chronicling our progress through the desert, but I never seem to find time to read the paper. Someday, when we get where we're going, I'll be grateful that he's written everything down. I hate to disappoint Andrew, but I shake my head from side to side and say, "No. I'm sorry, Andrew. I have not."

He tips his head forward. "Oh, I see."

A mother never misses a child's expression of disappointment. I return to mixing the cake and realize that he is waiting for me to ask him about the paper. I smile and make an inquiry, but can feel my smile melt when he tells me that he wrote a story about the Indian that follows us and how his sister has married the mystical shaman. I thank him for telling me and say, "I'm looking forward to reading it, Andrew."

As I set the cake at the edge of the fire, I tell myself that everyone was bound to find out today, anyhow. After all that we've been through together, from Independence to American Falls, maybe my fellow travelers have learned to expect the unexpected. Maybe they'll understand that things are different in the wilderness than in the cities and towns in which they grew up.

When the cake is finished, I put it in a covered box in the back of the wagon to cool. On the way to Reverend Meadows' Sunday services, I stop to read the newspaper. I slowly lower the flap on the post and gaze toward the Heavens. I pray that the optimistic words that flow from Andrew's young fingertips prove true.

Everyone stares as I join the assembled worshipers. My mind wanders as Reverend Meadows delivers a fiery sermon. When my fellow travelers join in song, it sounds like a choir of angels. After the conclusion of the open-air service, I turn away from the preacher, and Samuel Grosvenor appears at my side. Since Galusha got kicked in the head, Samuel has been forced to speak on his own behalf. He says, "Is it true? Your girl married a wild Indian?"

"I wish them nothing but great joy and happiness, Samuel."

"Indian lover!"

I lift my head high and say, "Be that as it may, Mr. Grosvenor." I lift Dahlia Jane from the ground and walk away.

This is not the first time I've been called such a name. When I was Rose's age, the boy I imagined to be my intended was half-Indian. My own brother, Erastus called me *Indian lover* so often, I began to regard it as a compliment. Why do I now find the words so troubling to my ear, all these years later?

Though Sunday is a day of rest, I spend most of the afternoon working in camp. I bake dozens of biscuits and scrub our clothes against the infernal washboard. A couple of passersby briefly manage to make eye contact, and others repeat Samuel's hateful words. I try to convince myself that I don't care what they think, but the heavy feeling of being judged weighs on my shoulders. I feel like Hardtack, pushing against the yoke.

I'm grateful to Cobb and his children who pass back and forth between Cobb's camp and mine as usual. Also, the scouts on the other side don't treat us differently. When Alvah and Lucky Nye stop by, Alvah says, "All the best to you and your daughter, Mrs. Moon," and Lucky nods agreement. Otherwise, everyone else avoids us, including the families who traveled with us since last year.

At dinner, Snarling Wolf faces the collective fire of questions from Andrew and Christopher. Between them, they manage to extract his life story. I'm pleased that the shaman patiently answers the boys as he fills their heads with galloping tales of life on the great plains.

When I serve my iced cake, Snarling Wolf licks sticky frosting from his thumb with a pop. His eyes grow wide and I wonder if the sweetness is a novelty for him.

As I rise to clean up after supper, The Committee arrives in camp and several passengers from the wagon train have followed. They waste no time making their purpose clear. Captain Meadows says, "How could you permit your daughter to marry this Indian, Mrs. Moon?"

I say, "What's done is done, Captain Meadows."

Samuel Grosvenor says, "He's a heathen and she's practically a child."

Dottie Crouse says, "It isn't right, Dorcas. Not without a church wedding. What if the Reverend performs a Christian marriage service?"

Snarling Wolf says, "We do not offer to marry in that way."

Dottie covers her gaping mouth with her hand. "He speaks English?"

Snarling Wolf points to Boss Wheel, who watches from his wagon. He says, "Ol' Wheel taught me."

Captain Meadows says, "I can't do anything about what happens out there," shaking his hands angrily in the direction of the Snake River. "Unless and until this man and this child are married before God, I'll not allow them to spend the night camped among us. Is that clear?"

The angry preacher's knobby nose twitches even though his harangue has ended. The cheeks on his flat face burn red in anger. He's clearly not accustomed to having his point of view opposed.

Snarling Wolf says, "We will live as Lakota. We are married before the eyes of the Great Spirit."

As I'm cleaning up after supper, I hear voices behind the master's wagon. I linger at the provision box for a moment.

Boss Wheel rants. Though his voice is gruff and scratchy, I can clearly hear his words. I wonder who he's talking to. "Every year, it is just the same. By the time we reach the Snake, everyone turns crazy. Plum loco. They're tired, cranky, and they've had their fill of each other. Problem is, they still have so far yet to go."

Agapito says, "The threat of outlaws makes it even worse, no?"

"Some days I think, if the outlaws don't get 'em, I'll kill the miserable greenhorns myself." A coughing fit ends their conversation and I wonder what preceded the part I overheard.

Monday, August 5

Following our day of rest, the groggy oxen lumber slowly along, and Hardtack, our steady, lead ox, stumbles when he pushes against the yoke. I had hoped that by now, the kine would regain some of the weight they had lost while pulling Larkin's safe. I thought the extra days at Fort Hall, and the grass we cut there would strengthen them, but it hasn't seemed to make a difference. It is not enough. Looking at their boney flesh makes me want to discard everything in our wagon. What else can we do to lighten our load?

After a couple of hours, the path wends through rocky terrain. Though it is early August, the brittle landscape looks as dry as autumn. Grass that must have once been green now stands brown and it is hard to differentiate from the umber stones.

Ancient-looking boulders frame a narrow passage along the trail. There's barely enough room for a wagon to fit through the opening. The wagons slow to a stop and then wait as the preceding travelers move slowly through the portal. The passageway is so narrow, it's hard to imagine fitting our rig through the opening.

The oxen bellow when Christopher snaps the whip above their heads. The chains jangle as the teams strain against their yokes and pull the wagon toward the aperture. When the lead oxen reach the gate, Christopher cusses loudly as Hardtack stumbles, drops to his knees, and keels over, pulling hard to the left. Scrapple struggles to remain on his feet as his partner forces the rig to lean leftward.

It takes a moment before I realize that I'm screaming. Men run toward our wagon as Andrew and Christopher bolt toward the fallen ox. I snatch Dahlia Jane from the ground and sweep her into my arms. I step forward and cover my mouth. I mustn't scream again for fear of further frightening the child.

Agapito and Arikta lead their horses toward Hardtack. Andrew and Christopher can't unhitch Hardtack by themselves. It's challenging enough to harness and unharness oxen when they are standing.

With the assistance of a dozen volunteers, Hardtack is released from his final burden. Then, Agapito and Arikta rope the dead animal and drag him through the rocky gate, to the other side. The remaining oxen seem to understand that they must go on without their leader.

As the wagon begins to roll again, tears flood from my eyes. Are animals capable of looking out for one another? Is it possible that Hardtack martyred himself to lighten the impact on his teammates?

Dahlia Jane tries to comfort me. "Hardtack's in Heaven now, Mama. Try not to be so sad." Her tiny hands pat my shoulders and I twist my head as far away from her as I can without dropping her.

"I know, dear. You're right, Dahlia Jane." I choke up between sentences. "I'll try my best, but it's very sad. Hardtack worked so hard for us."

"I know, Mama." She inhales in bursts and whimpers, "What will we do now?"

"Oh, honey. Scrapple and the others will have to go on without Hardtack, the best they can."

"Like we go on without Pa?"

"Yes, darling. I suppose so." But it's not the same. It's not the same when animals die as when we lose friends and family.

Charlotte reaches for Dahlia Jane. I tell my daughter that everything will be alright and watch as the woman takes the child to her wagon. Then, I make my way to Hardtack's side as wagons roll past us. I drop to my knees, spread my arms wide, and embrace the russet fur of my fallen hero. My chest feels heavy. I'm surrounded by a feeling of guilt. It's my fault that Hardtack is dead. Why didn't I dump that safe the first chance I got? Why didn't we listen to Boss Wheel and Agapito? I should never have let Larkin conceal it.

I don't have the power to stop my tears from flowing. My face is pressed into the thick neck of the stalwart steer. I almost suffocate myself for lack of air. I gasp as I sob, when I pull my head from Hardtack's furry neck. What does it say about me that I should hold my tears when my husband dies, and weep like an infant at the death of an ox?

When I finally straighten up and rub the tears from my cheeks, there's nobody else in sight. I turn and look through the Gate of Death. Everyone has made it through the rocky passage and I turn my back to it, looking westward, instead. The last of the wagons have disappeared around a bend in the trail. How long have I been blubbering like a child?

I blink quickly to clear my vision, look down, and notice that Hardtack isn't wearing Rose's sage necklace. He must have lost the protection that she thinks it offered and I frown at the idiocy of believing in such a talisman. Yet, I can't help thinking that he might still be alive if he hadn't lost it.

A man clears his throat behind me and I turn toward him.

Agapito hands me a handkerchief. His words match the expression on his face. "Pardon me, Dorcas. I am very sorry. I understand how you feel about animals. Especially, *el patrón*." He offers me his arm and says, "May I escort you back to your wagon, *estimada*?"

Dabbing my eyes with Agapito's handkerchief, I say, "I know I must seem foolish, to carry on so about an ox. Somehow, Hardtack felt like a member of the family." I stutter, "Everyone says they're dumb, but there was something about Hardtack that I just can't explain. It's like there was more to him than just another cow."

"Yes." Agapito gestures with his arm and looks back at the reddish-brown Devon. "Hardtack was not just another cow. He was *el patrón*, benevolent leader of animals. He has served you well. Remember him fondly." Agapito leads me away, across a small estuary named Fall Creek and then up a steep hill.

Our hopes and dreams now depend on Scrapple to lead the teams of oxen and I pray that he will be a worthy enough successor to Hardtack.

When the wagons circle, the scouts distribute fresh meat, and everyone seems to appreciate a rich repast.

TUESDAY, AUGUST 6

IN THE MORNING, LUCKY Nye appears beside my morning fire and thanks me for supper. I'm sickened to learn that we ate Hardtack last night. If I had known, I would have skipped our evening meal.

The children have made a pre-dawn trip to the river. The mountain man looks around, notices that we're alone, and crouches beside the fire. He gazes into the embers as he speaks and when he stops talking, I realize that I haven't been paying attention. He shifts his head to look at a space between me and the flickering flames.

"I'm sorry, Lucky. What did you say? I got to thinking about Hardtack and didn't hear what you said."

"Oh." He sounds disappointed, like he wishes he didn't have to repeat himself. "I was explaining that I'll be leaving tomorrow. I'll follow the trail south when we reach the Raft River."

I reach forward and place a hand on the man's shoulder. "I hoped that you would accompany us all the way to Oregon." I pause for a moment. I hope the answer to my question will be no, though the sentiment is selfish. "Is Alvah going with you?"

"No, ma'am... Dorcas. Alvah ain't certain he wants to settle in Oregon, but he reckons he'll finish what he started and he's keen on completing the journey."

"Where are you going?

"Remember I told you about my daughter, Bia Maswiki, who lives in a Lemhi village? I'm overdue and she worries when I'm gone too long."

"It must be hard having your children scattered throughout the wilderness."

"Yes. It would be easier if they lived together." Lucky's deep voice trails off quietly and makes me think of a withering fire.

"Have the girls met?"

"No."

"Have you told them?"

"Yes, they know about each other, but neither wants to meet the other."

"I'm surprised that you and Alvah will travel different paths. After a lifetime apart, I thought that you would become inseparable."

Lucky grips his thick knees tightly. "For the last five weeks, we have been. But Alvah is a grown man. He doesn't need me, but my girls do. It will be hard to part with my son. All these years, I always felt like something was missing. I didn't know what it was. Now I do." Lucky's voice catches in his throat as he says, "I'll never forget him." He turns his head away from me. I imagine his eyes filling with tears as he quickly blinks them away.

"Perhaps you'll meet again, Lucky."

"I sure hope so. We found each other once, maybe we can find each other again."

"We'll look after him for you." I move closer to him and my hand extends across his back. I pull him toward me in a sideways embrace.

I'm surprised when he shifts his position, turns fully toward me, wraps his arms around me, and plants his lips on mine. I'm even more shocked to find myself kissing him back, greedily, like lovers separated for far too long. I close my eyes and my heart races as his hands travel down my back. In my mind, I picture us together, but it isn't Lucky that I see. I feel my body tense and pull away from him. "I'm sorry, Lucky. I didn't mean to... I just wanted to tell you that we'd look after Alvah for you." Then I stand and say, "But more likely than not, Alvah will be looking after us." I offer my hands to help him up. His knees crack as he stands. "I'm so glad we found you, Lucky. We're going to miss you when you're gone."

When I release Lucky's hands and turn away from him to begin preparations for another day on the trail, I see Stillman standing a short distance away. It's still dark and I can't see the expression on his face, but he lingers, still as a statue, holding a big pail of water. I wonder how long he's been standing there.

Stillman sets the pail on the ground and stutters as he begins to speak. "I didn't mean to intrude. The children will be along in a moment."

I thank Stillman, wish him a good morning, and heft the pail to the water barrel on the wagon side. Stillman, Andrew, and Christopher harness the oxen and the animals don't seem to notice that they are missing a member of their team.

As we finish preparations for the day's journey, I'm conflicted. I am sure that I *would* enjoy slipping beneath Lucky's blankets in the middle of the night, but he isn't the man that my heart longs for. I can't help fantasizing about him, but I feel guilty about it. I could spend one night with such a man, but couldn't live with a man that struggles to talk to me and can't bring himself to look me in the eyes. Unwholesome thoughts are sometimes welcome, especially when they provide distraction from the hardships and dangers of a long journey through the wilderness.

I can feel the heat on my cheeks far too often as I think about Lucky Nye throughout the day. As the wagons circle into camp for the evening, my thoughts become more realistic. I'm not a young girl or a new bride. Such romantic notions are for youths, like Shakespeare's Romeo and Juliet. I'm too old for such distractions. My purpose is to keep my family safe and raise my children the best I can as a woman alone.

There's not much in the way of fertile meadows. Other than the grassy banks of Birch River, near the outlaws' cabin, there is a decent amount of grass along Monroe Creek, to the east.

Some wagons employ scouts who know how to find patches of grass, even in these high, arid plains. Looking through the spyglass, The Viper says, "This would be a good night for Indians to steal some oxen." Making their work look like it was done by Indians is one of The Viper's favorite tactics.

Everything goes according to plan. Using a bow and arrows, The Viper quickly dispatches two young guards who were supposed to ensure the safety of the oxen. Sloan and The Radish quietly herd the lumbering beasts up the quickly shrinking creek, through a ravine, and into the mountains.

Five well-mounted pilgrims gallop after the stolen oxen, brandishing guns and firing at anything that moves. Anything that's not an ox, that is. The brothers fire back, discarding the bow and arrows.

The outlaws are forced to abandon the mission and fan out through the uninhabited mountains. A bullet scraped The Viper's shoulder. He grits his teeth and steels his jaw against the pinching pain. His injured shoulder doesn't trouble him nearly as much as the fact that he doesn't know where his b rothers are.

After their troubles the previous year, The Viper was certain they had learned their lesson. This is their livelihood. They should be getting better at it, not worse. The Viper had been having second thoughts about retiring after this season. How can they fail to separate a few stupid oxen from their owners? Maybe it is time to quit living like this and take it easy. What if that bullet had killed him? Sloan and The Radish aren't smart enough to survive on their own. Leon is capable enough, but where is he? He should be back by now. The Viper's brothers don't even know where their money is hidden. Only the Viper knows. He smiles, picturing the many little nooks and crannies where The Viper has stowed the stolen treasures, dividing the money up between the wagons as if each one were a bank. It isn't smart to put all of one's money in ne place. It's safer to spread it around.

WEDNESDAY, AUGUST 7

IN THE MORNING, I spend a couple of hours carrying Jenny and walking with Stillman. The hardworking young man is unusually talkative today. He asks, "Are you in love with Lucky Nye?"

I shift Cobb's baby girl from one arm to the other and sigh. "No, Stillman. I must admit attraction and admiration, but it is not love."

"What I saw yesterday didn't mean anything?"

I glance at Stillman. "I wouldn't say that, Stillman. Lucky means a lot to me. We got swept away in a moment, but it was not enduring love. Do you understand?"

"I guess."

I turn slightly away and gaze off toward the mountains to the south. "Stillman, if you had to pick between a decade of ordinary, dependable love or one year of fierce, passion and true love, which would you choose?"

Stillman walks silently beside me and I wonder whether he's thinking about the answer or whether he'd prefer not to talk about such things. I turn back toward him and can feel my eyebrow lifting, as if compelling his response. He says, "Heck of a choice to have to make, wouldn't you say?"

The tail end of a snake disappears into the dried grass off to our left, but we walk forward without pause. I say, "Yeah. I don't think either of us made a choice, but you had one and I had the other." His cheeks flush bright red beneath his dark brown eyes.

"Does this subject make you uncomfortable, Stillman?"

"Sure does. I try not to think about such things let alone talk about them. It ain't no fun being... different."

"I think I understand. It must be very difficult. Perhaps in the distant past things were otherwise. I like to believe that in the future, such differences won't matter."

"But we don't live in the past or the future. If people knew about me, I'd get beat up, run off, or killed. You hear Reverend Meadows' sermons."

"I do. You're right to keep your secret to yourself, Stillman. But not everyone believes as Reverend Meadows does. There are others like you. Agapito says he's met others."

Stillman stops walking, covers his face with his hand and groans. Even with his face covered, his tortured expression is apparent. I want to inquire how he met Carter, but now is not the time. He gasps. "You told Agapito? Why? You promised."

"No, Stillman. I did not. *He* told *me* that he saw a silhouette of you and Carter in the wagon on the night Carter's hat was lost in the Kaw River. He has known for months, Stillman. Has he treated you any differently?"

Stillman looks at me with a painful grimace that melts my heart. He quietly tends to the needs of others without being asked or complaining, and I hate to see him suffer so. The young man strangely reminds me of Hardtack. Stillman says, "No. Don't tell him you told me. He won't say anything will he? If one more person finds out, I'm leaving. The pumas can eat me until I'm gone for all I care." He's silent for a moment, then blurts, "Sometimes I like to pretend I'm invisible."

"Wouldn't that be fun?" Without thinking, I say, "Just like a ghost!" I lower my voice to a whisper. "Oh, but I don't believe in such things. Anyway, I told you I won't tell anyone. And I'm glad you're not invisible, Stillman."

"Thanks, I reckon." After another quiet minute, Stillman says, "I'm glad you aren't in love with Lucky Nye."

"Good Heavens. Why?"

"You don't belong with him."

"Oh, I don't?" I look at the young man quickly, afraid he's going to ask me to marry *him* again. "Are you suggesting someone else would be better for me?"

"Of course. You're in love with Agapito and he feels the same way about you."

I shake my head, slap the boy on the back and he stumbles forward. I chuckle and whisper, "You may be half right, but don't go telling anyone my business, either. There's a bunch of reasons we can never be together."

"Hogwash."

"Oh Stillman, I'm too old for such foolishness. Nobody wants to marry an old lady with four children, let alone one who is practically six feet tall."

"Nonsense." I enjoy listening to Stillman's attempts to convince me otherwise, but my opinion remains unbudgeable. Eventually, he gives up and we walk quietly together for a while.

When I've almost forgotten that he's beside me, Stillman says, "Do you know all the terrible things people say about you?"

"Goodness gracious, Stillman. Whatever do you mean?"

"They call you names because you spend so much time with Cobb and his family. They call you other names because of Rose's...." He looks away and seems afraid to finish his sentence.

I say, "Husband? Snarling Wolf?"

"Yeah. And it's not just the Committee. I guess you know how Mr. Gains and Mr. Grosvenor feel, but it's not just them. I heard Esther and Addie talking about it too. They say you should stick with your own kind."

Anger builds within me. My hand finds my chin and I pinch it with my fingers, thinking about what to say to Stillman. Then, I realize that my chin smarts from gripping it too tightly. I think of all the things I've done for Esther and Addie and all the time we've spent together through the years. Then, I realize that Esther has barely spoken to me since Plumjohn was born. At least Addie is pleasant enough to me when we meet, but I can't remember a single time that she's walked over to our wagon. I must always go to her camp. In a blaze of clarity, I realize that the friends I grew up with aren't the friends who mean the most to me now. Finally, I say to Stillman,

"If they feel that way, then I guess *they* aren't my own kind. What do you think, Stillman?"

He says, "I agree with *you*. I don't know if I like Snarling Wolf, but I like the scouts, Cobb, and the Franklins."

"I'm glad. Despite what everyone seems to think, I don't suppose the color of one's skin has much to do with the kindness in their heart."

Our conversation ends as the wagons slow to a stop. Christopher runs toward us shouting. "We've reached the Parting of the Ways, Mama. Come quick."

We make our way to the junction where ruts diverge. One pair of wagon tracks continues west and the other turns south. Lucky and Alvah face each other, a few feet apart, and I'm reminded of the moment they met at Fort Bridger. I can't help approaching them. I tell myself that they should be alone in this moment, but everyone watches as father and son prepare to head in different directions. The stoic mountain man and his brave son appear emotionless, only I am close enough to see the subtle expressions on their faces.

Finally, Lucky says, "Write to me at Fort Bridger. Maybe I'll make my way to the coast in the spring." He blinks rapidly, reaches his hand forward, and I can hear the slap as their hands meet in a firm grip. Then, Lucky turns toward me, grips the rim of his hat and nods his head toward me. An instant later, he's headed south.

I watch him as he walks away. I can't help admiring his imposing figure as he moves. Despite his years, the man has powerful shoulders, a muscular back, narrow waist, and strong legs. He's the only man I've ever kissed who was taller than I am, not that I've kissed that many men. For a moment, in his arms, I felt attractive rather than awkward.

We're still watching when he turns toward us. He removes his hat, waves it in the air toward us in a final farewell. Then he swings his head and drops his hat over his straight, chestnut colored hair.

I turn toward Alvah and stretch my arms wide. He steps into my embrace and thanks me for comforting him. "I'll be alright, he says. Part of me wishes I could go with him." Alvah's body relaxes as he continues. "At Fort Bridger, it was like meeting a ghost, only he was real." The youngest Alvah Nye is quiet for a moment. Then, he says, "I don't know why, but I must continue on. I'm at home here with the wagon train. I just can't leave this journey unfinished. There's a reason I'm here and I don't know what it is. For a while, after we ran into him, I thought it was to find my father. Maybe that is part of what the fates had in store for me, but there's something else also. I just don't know what."

I offer, "Maybe you'll know it when you see it. Perhaps it will come to you at just the right moment. It would be very hard to say goodbye to you, Alvah."

As we conclude our embrace and separate, I realize that Christopher's good arm is wrapped around the small of Alvah's back. I know how special Alvah is to him, especially since he lost his Pa.

In a deep, quiet voice, Alvah says to me, "I've always felt like an invisible shadow. I don't feel like that anymore."

Thursday, August 8

THE DAYS SEEM TO be getting shorter and the mornings darker. At the same time, finding fodder for the morning fire seems to be getting more difficult. Buffalo chips are in short supply and wood is almost non-existent. It's all I can do to make coffee by burning sprigs of greasewood and sage.

Agapito passes through camp with a grunt. "Dry camp tonight. Nothing to burn. Fill the barrels with water and if you find anything to burn along the way, grab it."

I offer him a cup of coffee and he declines. I try to make conversation, but he doesn't look at me when I speak to him. Instead of facing me, he looks toward Cobb's wagon, nearby. Agapito seems more like Lucky than himself today. With the backs of his hands resting on his slender hips, Agapito says, "*Perdóname*, I must spread the word. It will be a long day."

As the assistant wagon master saunters away, I wonder what's gotten into him. He's never been too busy to exchange pleasantries before. Perhaps Boss Wheel's pessimism has rubbed off on the man. Maybe he's as worried as everyone else about the dangers that lie ahead. He could just be having a bad day. Everyone is entitled to feeling out of sorts now and again—why not Agapito?

When the wagons begin to roll, Andrew appears beside me. I ask, "Any rain today?"

"No, Mama, today's going to be sunny and hot."

"Agapito says we're going to have a dry camp tonight."

"Yes, Mama. Mr. Franzwa says we'll leave the Snake for a couple of days."

As the day progresses, we seem to be losing ground. The master's wagon pulls farther ahead every hour. It's as if Agapito is trying to increase the distance between us. I try to convince myself that I'm being ridiculous. If anything, our oxen are falling behind because we've only got two teams pulling instead of three. I bemoan the loss of Hardtack. Scrapple and the others must do the best they can to keep up.

It's a dry day and the surroundings are unpleasant. I don't know whether it is in fact the hottest day of the year, but it feels as if it is. There's scarcely any sort of vegetation for miles in any direction, and no water. Even sage is hard to find. I find myself bending over and plucking the smallest bits of combustible material from the ground, and after hours of searching, I've only managed to accumulate a couple of handfuls of dried leaves and twigs in the bottom of a bag, and nary a buffalo chip. I remember Agapito's words this morning: "It will be a long day."

It occurs to me that I should ride rather than walk, but I don't feel like it. I'm sure that it would improve my mood, but maybe I don't feel like being cheerful today. Some days are like that.

As I walk along, leaving the oxen to the boys, my mind drifts back to Lucky's embrace. My fingers gently touch my lips and it is almost as if I can still feel his strong hands on the small of my back. I was married for a long time, but I had never been kissed like that before. When the muscular nomad wrapped his arms around me, an excitement I haven't felt in years pulsed through my body, and yet, when I closed my eyes, it wasn't the modest mountain man whose face I saw. Instead, it was the cheerful Mexican guide I pictured, and it was him that I was thinking of when I kissed Lucky back as if I had waited for that moment my whole life.

Why can't I set foolish, romantic notions aside? Lucky is a good man. Agapito is a treasured friend. That's all there is to it. I remind myself that I'm too old to go on behaving like I did when I was a young girl. I take a deep breath and am transported back through the years to the cool mountain forests and my endless, pointless pursuit of the half-Mohawk boy of my dreams. Even now, after all of these years, just the thought of Noah causes me to melt and wish that life could have turned out differently. Instead, he disappeared and I married his best friend, Larkin. Then he reappeared and married Arminda. I think of Agapito again and wonder, if I could choose between them, which man would I choose, Noah or Agapito?

I stop for a moment and stomp my foot. I tell myself, *That's enough, Mustang Moon. Pull yourself together.* I shake my head at the foolishness of my thoughts. Good Heavens, I hope that nobody is watching me. I must look as nutty as Rose, the way I'm carrying on.

And yet, my thoughts return to an impossible choice, though both alternatives are absurd. But what if I could spend one night with one or the other? My idea of Noah has lived deep in my heart for decades. Through the years, I've convinced myself that I should be ashamed that I tried to push myself on him. When I'm honest with myself, I regret not having seduced him more thoroughly. I had more than one opportunity to throw caution to the wind. He would have been powerless to resist.

Yet now, all these years later, the exotic, confident man with the friendly demeanor excites me more. Whenever he's near, I can't help following him with my eyes. I try my best to pretend otherwise, but seek excuses to be near him. I think about him whenever we're separated. Though I constantly tell myself there's no chance for us to be together, I remain a dreadfully poor listener.

I've memorized the many reasons we can't be together and recite them often in my head. First, he's a Mexican and I'm not, not that I give a rip what people think about that. Secondly, Boss Wheel doesn't allow his crew to frolic with the emigrants, though I can't help wondering whether *that* rule has been broken in the past. And then, there's Agapito's promise to Merced. That's before considering that I'm taller than he is, and older as well. Berta is pretty, young, and virginal. That's the sort of woman men prefer, confound it. I'm sure Agapito and Berta will begin courting the minute the wagon train reaches Oregon. Besides, what man would want to raise another man's family?

I don't know how many times I've told myself; I'm destined to be a woman alone. I must be father and mother to my children. From now on, I will commit to avoiding my temptation. The less time spent with Agapito, the better.

FRIDAY, AUGUST 9

A COUPLE OF HOURS after departing our camp near the confluence of the Snake and Raft Rivers, Charlotte wanders back from her wagon to visit with us as she walks. She chatters about the newlyweds who travel with her and Hollis, and often makes remarks about what Martin would have thought of every subject she mentions. I know that's her way of keeping her son alive. Before long, the doctor's wife talks wistfully about leisurely afternoons in her Virginia parlor. Charlotte turns her head, looks into my face and says, "It seems like that was a different lifetime from this one. I'm beginning to think we'll never get anywhere. It wouldn't surprise me if we spent forty years wandering in the wilderness, just as Moses did before reaching the Promised Land. Oregon is for future generations, not me and Hollis."

"*Poco a poco se anda lejos.*"

Charlotte casts a quizzical glance at me and I repeat the proverb, only louder and then translate it. "Little by little, one goes far. Agapito says this from time to time. We must have faith. If we keep marching, we shall finally reach our destination."

"From your lips to God's ear, Dorcas. I never expected to walk so much. I thought we would ride on the wagon instead of walking beside it. If only I had paid more attention to people when they talked about going to Oregon."

When we stop at an inhospitable location, devoid of landmarks or waterways, most travelers prepare a light meal or sit a spell. Charlotte visits with the children and I step to the top of a minor butte, a couple of hundred yards to the south of the trail. It's too hot for unnecessary exertion, but the urge to see something new is irresistible.

Not really expecting to see anything different, but hopeful nevertheless, I step slowly to the top of the rise carrying the rifle in my right hand. Just over the hill, half a dozen wolves quarrel over the dead body of a horse, large enough to feed them all. It is just like a scene from one of my nightmares, only it is the middle of the day. I should back away and return to the safety of our wagons, but instead, my body freezes in place. It is the last thing I ever hoped to see, yet I am powerless to look away. The canines yip, snarl, growl, and whine as they yank hunks of bloody red flesh from the fallen mustang. Did the horse die naturally or did the pack of wolves run the wild horse down before ripping it to shreds? Its head is untouched and the panic in its eyes remains evident.

I imagine the terror the animal experienced as it met its grisly end. One of the canines turns away from its feast and spies me. From twenty yards away, its ears stand erect, pointed slightly forward and I can hear the low, rumbling growl even over the noise made by its slobbering packmates. If the beast wanted to attack me, it could easily reach me in a matter of seconds. I might have time to get the rifle in place and fire a shot, but the way my hands shake, I couldn't be sure of my aim. Having made eye contact with the largest wolf I've ever seen, and from a closer distance than I've ever imagined, my feet find the power to propel me backward.

Without turning my back on the site of the carnage, I make my way slowly back toward the wagon train as my fellow passengers prepare to renew their daily march. Charlotte tries to speak to me, but all I'm able to do is blink rapidly. Her eyes look at my chin which shakes like it might if today were the coldest day of the year rather than one of the warmest. Finally, I'm able to compose myself enough to tell her what I saw over the butte's crest.

We walk in silence for a mile or two and finally, Charlotte asks about the Banyons. "How's Cobb getting on with the baby and the children, Dorcas?"

Her inquiry reminds me that I wanted to ask her if she could fashion some clothes for young Joe. "They're getting on the best they can. I don't know how Cobb manages, and we help when we can. Cobb wants to breech the boy, though Joe is only three. He asked if I knew where he could find a set of clothes for him. I told him I would see what I could do, but you know how I hate to sew."

It is as if Charlotte has temporarily forgotten the ordeal of long distance travel. A conspiratorial glimmer in her eye reveals her gleeful thoughts as she says, "I'll see what I can come up with."

A couple of minutes later, Charlotte bids us adieu and steps back toward her wagon with a spring in her step. After the wagons circle up, chores are done, and the supper dishes are stowed back in the wagon. Charlotte appears beside our campfire. Andrew stands and offers her his seat on a box next to me.

The woman looks happy yet melancholy at the same time. After she sits and lets a big breath escape her lungs, she pulls carefully folded clothes from a sack she carried with her. "I don't know why I saved these. Of all the things to hold on to." She strokes the small folded shirt on the top of the stack as if reminiscing. "I was heartbroken when Martin insisted on dressing like his father. I wanted to keep him as a child for as long as I could, but he was stubborn about it. Finally, Hollis convinced me it was time. Martin wasn't much bigger than Joe, so I figure these'll do for him. I was saving them for my grandbabies."

Charlotte looks at me, raises her eyebrows and her lips bunch. "I don't need these keepsakes to think about Martin." She glances away and speaks into the gloaming. "So much death. There's horror at every turn of the trail." With a sudden sense of urgency, Charlotte thrusts the handful of clothes into my lap. "I want Joe to have them." She stands quickly, runs her hand slowly down her right cheek, and adds, "There. That's done." As she turns and hurries away, she wishes me a good night.

When I close my eyes as our encampment settles in after dark, I think about how hard it must have been for Charlotte. Martin was in his prime, just on the brink of adulthood. What might he have made of his life if it weren't for the tragic accident, or desperate action, that killed him before he could find his way? Will it be hard for Charlotte to see young Joe wearing Martin's clothing?

Martin's trousers and vest are the same color as the liver chestnut mustang that the wolves feasted on today. Sleep is hard to come by with thoughts of sharp-toothed canines niggling in my brain.

Saturday, August 10

It's getting late in the day, and naturally, thoughts turn to settling in for the evening. We were told to expect a nice campground along Duck Creek, and that we would cross the creek before circling for the evening. So it is a surprise when the caravan comes to a stop without circling. Curiosity gets the better of me, and I head forward on foot to see what has halted our forward progress.

Our position in line is rather far back, so it takes me a while to hotfoot it past two thirds of the procession. I cringe at the sound of a barking dog, but it doesn't slow my pace. Who is in the leadoff spot today? It's hard to keep track, since it changes every day. My hand covers my mouth when I see Landon and Cornelia Young's rig tipped into a hole.

Several men work to help Landon unhitch his oxen as the beasts fight to free themselves. Women gather and watch, many holding small children as I dash past them and pull a shovel from the side of the Young's wagon and join a group of men working to dig a slope so that unencumbered oxen can step from the crater.

After an hour, five of Landon's six oxen have been rescued from the depression. The sixth has a broken leg.

I turn my back and brace myself for the sound as Boss Wheel puts the poor creature out of its misery. Still, I jump as the gun fires and hear the thud of the ox dropping to the ground as I turn back toward the men. Boss Wheel places a hand on Landon's shoulder and says, "That was a fine animal. He served you well, son. I'm sorry this happened to you." He lets go of the young man, steps closer to the deep hole, and rubs his whiskery chin. "In all my years, I never seen anything like this. I guess, as they say, there's a first time for everything."

Agapito hastily organizes volunteers and a team of oxen to tow the sunken prairie schooner from the sinkhole. Then, with a sweep of his arm, Boss Wheel tells the gathered crowd to help Landon get his team hitched back to the front of his conveyance. The young man still looks stunned as he turns to me and says, "We were just plodding along and then suddenly, the ground gave way beneath our feet." Landon drapes his arm over Cornelia's shoulder and she clutches three-year-old Junior to her chest.

The woman shakes her head slowly and says, "We sure are a long way from Falls Village, Connecticut. We never bargained for this."

The Franzwa family follows Landon and Cornelia Young, and the Franzwa children scramble to help gather up the Young's possessions which have tumbled from the corner of the vehicle and fallen from the hooks on its exterior.

Agapito speeds past us and says, "Return to your wagons. In a few minutes, we will return to the trail."

Obediently, I hasten back to our place in line and quickly relay the story to Stillman and my wide-eyed children. "Boss Wheel says this is the first time he's ever seen a sinkhole try to gobble up a load of greenhorns. You just never know what's going to happen next."

When we march past the pit, the boys are curious to look down into the hole, but Arikta has been stationed beside it. The scout shoos us along. "It is just a hole. Keep your distance." With both hands, he makes a sweeping motion and a few minutes later, we've passed the scene. An hour later, we trudge through a modest creek, and circle up on the other side.

It seems like ages since we've had such a pleasant place to camp. We could hardly call it a forest, but there are enough shrubs to make it feel at least somewhat hospitable. An impressive mountain to the south gives the eye something to feast on as we settle in.

After supper, I briefly visit next door. Cobb gratefully accepts Charlotte's gift. He appears sad and I wonder if he's thinking of Martin as he holds the hand-me-down clothing. Before stepping away, I tell Cobb that we can make modifications if the clothes don't fit Joe. Cobb asks me if we will stop by for a breeching ceremony after tomorrow's Sunday services. I tell him that we would love to, and hurry back to camp.

It's been ages since I've bathed or had a change of clothes. Duck Creek isn't deep enough to submerge, but it's far more generous than a trickle. It shall have to do. I quickly gather soap, a towel, and my spare clothing, and then scamper to the waterway. Soon it will be dark and I don't want to miss my chance. After a quick glance about, I'm confident that I'm alone. I disrobe, leaving my dirty clothes in a heap and splash into the knee-high water.

Though I carefully checked the riverbank, I neglected to make sure that nobody was in the water. We're both naked and I can't help staring. I yammer, "Goodness gracious. I'm ever so sorry. I didn't realize you were here, dear." The petite, blue eyed, blond haired German girl's figure is so arresting, it is hard to imagine that any man could resist her allure. No woman should have to stand near her, fully clothed, let alone stark naked.

"I vas jusht vinishink." She turns her back to me, bends over, and splashes herself.

I can't help staring at her full, round caboose. It's a wonder that she hasn't found a beau and turned him into a husband already. I turn my back to Berta, wishing I had the water hole to myself and begin to bathe. After a minute, she wishes me a good night and splashes past me. When she's gone, I admonish myself. What is it about this woman that turns my gills green with envy? If I were a man, I am sure that I would find her adorable.

Envy and jealousy are unbecoming traits and I like to think they are beneath me, but something about that girl brings out the worst in me. It would be a struggle to recall having ever had a conversation with her longer than the words we shared at the side of the creek tonight. She's probably a kind and warm-hearted person. I remind myself that not that long ago, her father was gored to death by a buffalo. She could probably use a friend. Berta doesn't deserve the unkind thoughts that cross my mind.

SUNDAY, AUGUST 11

A HOT WIND IS nevertheless a wind, and it offers some relief from the heat. Many of the men complain that we'll get stuck in the Blue Mountains if we don't quicken our pace and it is hard to imagine freezing while sweating, sitting still.

Several of us have gathered at The Hub and Luella snips hair without complaining about the wind currents. Travis Latham squirms while she works, stretching his jaw and complaining about his toothache.

Nearby, Hollis Appleyard says, "That's been bothering you since we left Independence. That's four months you've been suffering."

"Four months, you say? More like four years."

Travis's wife, Catherine says, "Listen to the cantankerous old bear carry on. Travis is prone to exaggeration. Four years, indeed. It started just before we joined the wagon train." She twists her long, straight hair in her hand.

Travis says, "My pretty wife is prone to minimizing things. I was complaining about this durn molar on my birthday when I turned thirty and that was over two years ago."

Hollis interrupts. "Why don't you let me pull that rotten tooth? It's got to come out, one way or another, whether you like it or not."

Travis protests, "I would, but I'm afraid I'd bite you, or worse, shoot ya. I like you, Doc. I wouldn't want to have to do that."

Hollis isn't the only one to chuckle, but Travis insists that he isn't joking.

Catherine asks Hollis if he could do it now and Travis groans.

Hollis asks if Travis has any whiskey.

"Nope, never touch the stuff. Don't believe in it."

Catherine reminds Hollis that they belong to Captain Meadows' church and that Travis is a Committeeman.

"That's right. Gotta set a good example."

Hollis says, "Suit yourself. I'll bring a jug in case you change your mind."

Luella finishes Travis' haircut and starts working on five-year-old Lem Latham's curly blond mop. Travis pays the Reverend's wife, thanks her for the hair cut, and says, "I best be skedaddling on out of here. I think I got something needs doing."

Catherine challenges her husband. "I thought you wanted to set a good example. What are Lucy and Lem supposed to think if you skip out on the doctor?"

Travis growls again and holds his jaw like his molar is on fire. "Confound it. How'm I gonna chew my food if I let that sawbones yank my teeth out?"

The farmer from Indiana shrinks as if trying to disappear as Hollis makes his way back from his wagon with his doctor's bag and a wooden box. "Have a seat, son." Hollis pulls a small jug from his bag and says, "Last chance." The doctor looks at the preacher's wife and says, "Captain Meadows and God will permit the indulgence, for medicinal purposes."

Travis sneers, takes the jug, pulls the cork, and draws a swig, swallowing hard. His eyes water, his fist thumps his chest, and he coughs heartily before drawing another mouthful of rotgut. The patient removes his pistol from its holster and passes it to the doctor. "Put this out of reach, will ya, Doc?"

Hollis scoffs, "You're not going to shoot me, Travis."

Lem's haircut is half finished, but Luella sets down her shears and watches. I'm amazed at the size of the forceps Hollis pulls from his bag. I can't imagine it fitting in poor Travis' mouth.

"Sit still, son. Somebody help me hold the man down. Catherine? Dorcas?"

It takes both of us to get the job done. Fortunately for Travis, Hollis is experienced at such extractions. The blackened tooth is forcefully yanked in one strong pull.

I've never heard such an ear-shattering sound as the deafening shriek Travis makes. It's a sound that could wake the dead and summon the Devil. The grown man rolls from the box, onto the ground, and writhes like a serpent, whimpering and holding his jaw.

Hollis extends a hand and helps Travis to his feet. "It will take some getting used to the fact that tooth is missing. It'll hurt for a while, but you should start feeling better in a couple of hours." He holds the jug up and says, "If you need a little bit more medicine, stop by the wagon."

Travis groans while Luella finishes Lem's haircut, then I help Catherine escort her husband back to their wagon. By the time we get there, Travis, says, "Quit babying me. I'll be fine." He nods at me and winks, then sits in the shade beneath their wagon and stretches out on his back. His son and daughter crawl in next to him and tickle his ribs.

I return to our wagon and am glad to find that Rose has joined us for the afternoon. Perhaps Snarling Wolf is off hunting or something. I gather the family and we step over to Cobb's wagon. I've got a small basket of baked goods and wish I could bring more. Eggs are hard to come by when you only have one laying hen.

Ever active, Bess and Joe chase each other around until Cobb summons the children, baby Jenny tucked into the crook of his arm. I trade Jenny for the basket of treats as the children sit with their legs crossed beside the fire.

Cobb says to Joe, "Are you ready for grown up clothes, young man?" The boy nods three times and his eyes flash proudly.

The father turns to us and says, "We'll be back in a minute or two."

While humming to the sleeping infant in my arms, I take a seat beside the campfire, facing the wagon and next to Rose.

When Cobb and Joe emerge from the back of the wagon, the three-year-old seems to be a foot taller than he looked going in. Instead of being dressed like a baby, the boy looks like a smaller image of his father.

I can't help but notice Rose as she looks back and forth from the provision box nailed to the wagon's side and the boy and his father a few feet away from us. Rose turns her head and an expression of deep sympathy softens her normally bleak cheeks. She turns her chin slightly toward me and whispers softly, "Jennie is proud of her little man. She can't believe a white woman from Virginia would do this for her family. She is grateful to Charlotte and to you. You have made her very happy, Mama."

Monday, August 12

Whereas other days have been hot, today seems to outdo all those that have come before. Often, while traveling, we have found it cool in the morning and then heat develops throughout the day. Today, it's a scorcher from the outset.

The scouts pass through camp early this morning with the news, "Dry camp tonight. Fill your barrels now. Does anybody need help?"

As we carry buckets of water from Duck Creek to fill the barrel strapped to the wagon, I ask Andrew, "Any relief on the way?"

"No, Mama. No end in sight. Today's going to be the worst day yet."

"I was afraid of that."

Before the wagons roll out, I insist everybody drink until they can't drink anymore and I bring extra to the stock. It would be a good day to sit still beside the trail and wait for cooler weather, but we sat still yesterday.

Andrew says, "Saddle up and ride Blizzard today, Mama. Dahlia Jane can ride in the wagon."

I agree and climb into the saddle. Normally I'd be tempted to ride off alone, but it's too hot to make Blizzard go anywhere unnecessarily. After a couple of hours, I notice that it is abnormally quiet. It occurs to me that nobody says anything. It's not just my family, but I don't hear anyone in nearby wagons either. We're like a clatter of ghosts marching toward that fiery hell Captain Meadows talks about on Sundays.

Though I would rather sit still and save my strength, I begin to think of friends and fellow travelers. After making sure that Stillman, Dahlia Jane, and the boys have had plenty of water, I nudge Blizzard forward and ride past the other wagons. Few people greet me with more than a grunt or nod. Ten wagons forward, I notice that Minor Shaw doesn't look too good.

"G'day sir, are you doing okay?" Minor is our oldest traveler, and his wife, Ellenanne worries about him. They're from Portsmouth, New Hampshire, and he was once a shipbuilder. When their daughter, Hetty, and her husband, Lloyd Carpenter decided to set out for Oregon, they chose to make the trip also.

Minor rubs his temples and says his head aches something fierce. He frowns and grumbles, "I wish it would rain." His hand pulls a damp neckerchief from a shirt pocket and he dabs his sweaty forehead. "I've had worse days, I guess."

"Do you need some water?"

"Got some right here."

I offer to walk with his oxen for a little while if he'd like to take a break, but the man thanks me and declines.

Three wagons beyond Minor Shaw, Travis Latham plods along beside his oxen while Catherine walks behind the wagon, where she can see Lucy and Lem in the back.

I inquire, "How's the toothache, Mr. Latham?"

"I don't know about that, but my head aches, I'm light headed and I feel like I could hork. I knew I shouldn't touch that liquor yesterday. I just wish this day would end."

"Make sure you drink a lot of water."

Travis lifts his hand as if waving slightly to indicate that he has heard me and will heed the warning. On days like this, it takes a lot of energy to voice a thought or lift a limb. And, hot as it is, each hour that goes by, it manages to get hotter still.

A couple of wagons farther on, the blacksmith's wife, Indiana Bellows looks peaked. They have the good fortune of being just before Alvah Nye, but today, it seems neither Alvah, nor Indiana's husband, Foster have noticed the present state of the wilting woman's condition. Like me, the young woman doesn't want to burden the oxen, but given my nature and my worries that she might faint, I insist she climb aboard with her son, Race, short for Horace. I make the five-year-old boy promise to look after his mother.

Instead of riding back to our place in line, I stand still and let our wagon catch up, and then I ride back a few wagons to check on those behind us. Everyone looks well enough, including the pregnant newlyweds, Serena Bond and Drucilla Horton. If anyone looks like they are suffering, it is the blond haired hothead, Wayne Horton, who looks like the sweltering heat is getting the better of him.

"Are you alright, Wayne?"

"It sure is hot, ain't it, Miss Dorcas?" He walks like his legs are too stiff to bend.

"You don't look too good. Something wrong with your legs?"

"Just a little stiff and sore. I'll be fine." Wayne yawns like he could fall asleep while walking in the middle of the day.

"Can I get you some water?"

To placate me, he makes a show of taking a big dipper full of water from the keg strapped to the side of his moving wagon and chugging it down.

Serena and Drucilla walk together between their wagons and do their best to keep their steps within the shade of the wagon covers, but soon the sun will peak, making shade scarce. If it's this hot before dinner, it's hard to imagine what's in store for us during the peak heat of the afternoon.

On my way back to my family's place in line, I pass Agapito and Arikta who are also checking up on the passengers. I tell them we are lucky to have signed up with an outfit that looks after its passengers and thank them for watching over us.

When we stop for the evening, I walk with Andrew to The Hub and hold the post as he pounds it into the dry dirt. At the side of a wagon, I see a man collapse. I point and shout. "Man down."

A slow-moving crowd gathers beside Minor Shaw's wagon. Arikta takes control of the situation. "Get the doctor." The Pawnee scout unbuttons the man's shirt and drags him into the shade beside his wagon. "Can you get me some rags, Mrs. Shaw?" I should help, but the young man seems to have the situation under control. The older man is conscious, but disoriented. Arikta douses the cloths with water and slops them onto Minor's wrists, ankles, neck, and forehead.

When Hollis arrives on the scene, he tells us all to return to our families and make sure everybody is alright while he and Arikta tend to Minor Shaw. Hollis mutters, "Maybe we should travel at night and stay still during the daytime."

TUESDAY, AUGUST 13

TUESDAY, IT SEEMS, IS just as hot as Monday was. Agapito insisted that Arikta drive Minor Shaw's oxen today, while the old shipbuilder recovers in his wagon. Indiana Bellows has also been ordered to ride, not walk. When the wagons circle for the evening, I ride around the perimeter and notice Wayne Horton on his knees, puking up what looks like gallons of water. Instead of rushing to his side, I hurry to Hollis' wagon and tell him what I observed.

When I follow the doctor back to Wayne's wagon, he says, "We need to cool that boy down." Hollis looks around urgently and says, "Can we use your horse, Dorcas?"

I nod, emphatically. "Yes, but I need to stay with you. Otherwise, Blizzard will pitch him to the ground."

Frightened Drucilla says, "Will he be alright, Doctor?"

Hollis tries to reassure Wayne's wife.

"You've just gotta save him." The twisted expression on her face looks desperate. It's bad enough being a widow on the trail, but I can't imagine being an eighteen-year-old, pregnant widow.

Wayne says, "If I gotta go, I'd rather this than being shot."

Drucilla barks. "Don't talk like that. I can't stand it." Then she pleads, "What can I do, Doc?"

Hollis tells Drucilla that she mustn't worry and that we'll take good care of her husband. There isn't much substance to the Pennsylvanian. He's like a child's picture of a stick figure. Still, it takes some effort to shove him from the ground onto the saddle, but between me and Hollis, we manage to heft Wayne onto Blizzard's back.

The short trip seems to take a long time, hot and tired as we are. As we reach the Snake River, Wayne's friend, Bobby jogs up to us and he helps us pull Wayne from the saddle. Bobby's wife, Serena is right behind him and she helps comfort Drucilla.

Hollis says, "Lay him down at the edge of the river."

Wayne blinks rapidly as the water surrounds him. His head is propped on the riverbank. The shore is like a pillow and he doesn't move for a minute. Suddenly, he sits up and convulses. He rolls over onto all fours and tries to vomit, but nothing comes up. After vomiting loads of water earlier, there isn't anything left to expel.

Hollis advises, "Stay with him. Keep him in the water, but don't let him drown. When his body cools, you should be able to get him to drink, but start with little sips. I'll be back in a while to check on you."

The doctor returns to camp, walking slowly, and sends as many people as he can convince, to join us in the river. Andrew tells me, "Dr. Hollis said everybody is overheated and we all need a good soaking. Then, we need to drink as much water as we can."

Usually when folks gather at a swimming hole, they raise a ruckus, frolicking in the water, and splashing all about. Today, everybody just sits, motionless in the river, praying for an end to the hot spell that will not seem to let up.

Sloan whines at The Viper. "It's too hot out today. Let's leave the pilgrims to suffer in the heat. We don't have to put them out of their misery today, do we? Couldn't we just rest in the shade, instead?"

The Viper snaps. "The season is going by fast and we are way behind. If you want to retire, we gotta make the most out of the time we got. At most, we've got a month left before the season is over."

The Radish spots a small string of wagons. "Look. What do you make of that? Seven wagons, maybe?"

The Viper hisses through his teeth. "Idiots. Give me that spyglass."

Sloan looks at his brother, surprised. "Isn't that what we want? Idiots?"

The Viper blasts, "Of course it is. Don't be stupid. How did such a small train get this far? They don't deserve to make it to Oregon. If we don't get 'em, something else will."

The Radish says, "Maybe they think seven is a lucky number."

The Viper spits. "No telling what these dunderheaded fools think." The Viper imagines the greenhorns slobbering and begging for their lives as he slices their throats and scrapes their scalps with his sharp blade.

"Can I have one of the women? Please, Lennox?" The Radish almost never calls The Viper by his given name.

"No. Probably not. You don't want a dead one, do you?"

The Radish makes a sour face. "No. I don't want a dead woman. Sheesh."

"I told you to wait until the season is over. There'll be plenty of time for that when we leave the outlaw trail. But mark my words. You'll find out for yourself. Women ain't nothing but trouble, kid."

The Radish shakes the buckle of his gun belt, moans mournfully, and his eyes roll.

The Viper tells The Radish, "Quit daydreaming. We've got work to do."

Two hours later, the brothers separate the back three wagons from the first four. The Radish chases the front four up the trail as Sloan disarms the young families in the last three wagons. The Viper toys with his victims, making them believe that they have some hope of surviving their ordeal, even as he slays beloved members of their families before their eyes.

The travelers in the first four wagons wail in fear of what has happened to their fellow emigrants. The survivors include four young men and two older ones. Three remain to protect their families, huddled in fear along the banks of the Snake, while the other three set off to rescue their lost friends.

The Radish fires his rifle into the air, alerting his brothers, but Sloan and The Viper are already on their way. The brave heroes that set out to save their friends don't survive the first volley of gunfire. An hour later, the families they left beside the Snake are also gunned down.

It takes the outlaws all night to shuttle the wagons, dead bodies, and stolen stock to their compound up Birch Creek.

WEDNESDAY, AUGUST 14

OUR PRAYERS GO UNANSWERED. Maybe today is a *little* cooler than Monday and Tuesday were, but it's still blazing hot. Marching through scorching days earlier in our journey was unbearable enough, but the relentless heat this week exceeds anything I can ever recall. I imagine what it might feel like to be baked in an oven and that's what comes to mind. Today's march felt like it took a week to get from morning to evening.

Yesterday, at the end of the day, poor Wayne Horton was overheated and nauseous. Today as we set up camp, half a dozen travelers suffer as Wayne did. Yesterday, we were able to cool Wayne by soaking him in the Snake River. Today, our encampment perches near the edge of a perilous cliff, making the river inaccessible. Our only hope is to cool ourselves with hot barrel water drizzled over washcloths as we pray for a break in the weather. We must also be careful not to deplete our water supply.

As I stand high above the river, dangerously close to the drop off, Arikta briefly joins me. He points over the embankment and tells me to look closely. "There is a forty foot waterfall and an angry pool. It is called Caldron Linn. The river gets mighty riled up down there."

"I'd like to get a better look at that."

"It is not possible. It is not safe to go down there from here. Only from the other side."

My imagination will have to do and I think of an evil witch stirring a poisonous concoction in a big black cauldron.

The scorched earth in this vicinity is so cooked that it rises as we travel across it. During our travels, a billowing cloud follows us, kicked up by our movement and looks like a giant tail rising hundreds of feet into the air. My fellow travelers look as if they have been dunked in buttermilk and rolled in flour, like raw chicken fit to be fried. The infernal dust fills our eyes with its grittiness, turning them red, and making us look like demons. Judging by the appearance of my fellow travelers, I'd hate to look at myself in a mirror.

As the sun edges closer to the horizon, a thin pillar of dust on the horizon indicates that someone is heading in our direction. A small crowd gathers to greet an incoming rider. He's a middle-aged fellow with a bushy white beard and a capote that looks like the one Boss Wheel wears. The man is far from friendly and dismounts with a groan. He discourages questions and conversations and looks around as if searching for somebody.

Agapito makes his way through the crowd, stepping forward, and pumps the man's hand briskly. "I do not believe my eyes. I heard you got killed. ¿Neta? I did not think it could be true." Speaking to Dembi Koofai, Agapito says, "Get Boss Wheel and tell him Pell-mell Dell is here." He calls for Arikta, and says, "Put up this old man's horse."

The assistant wagon master leads the visitor to his camp and the little gathered crowd begins to disperse. Nearby, Galusha Gains sputters unrepeatable words and ends his tirade with, "Damn foreigners." Galusha Gains has made himself scarce since he got kicked in the head and, evidently, the mustang's hoof didn't knock any sense into him. To Galusha, anyone outside of our rolling village is a foreigner.

I meander back to our wagon and arrive in time to overhear a rowdy reunion next door. Where do they come up with the energy for such enthusiasm? Normally, we're careful to maintain whatever energy we can muster in the midst of the heat spell.

My shoulders press into the back corner of our wagon and I rest my arm on the keg of water. Should anyone ask what I'm doing, my answer would be relaxing in the shade. I've learned that it is a good place to overhear conversations next door.

From what I can piece together, Pell-mell Dell was once a mountain man, like Boss Wheel, and they enjoy reminiscing about rendezvous gatherings. Before long, their vigorous reunion settles down and turns serious. Pell-mell Dell carries messages and mail between Fort Boise and Fort Hall. He warns of danger ahead. "You must be vigilant. We aren't sure whether we're dealing with a single gang of outlaws, several bands of renegades, or something even worse. It is hard to tell exactly what we're up against out here. I ought to just go to Saint Louis and set a spell rather than ride around out here anymore. I'm getting way too old for this sort of nonsense."

Though I'd prefer to linger and listen longer, it's time to settle the children in for the night. I'd love to hit the sack myself, but I am on watch from dark to midnight and wonder who else is on duty tonight.

My partner for the evening is Roy Franklin, which is good news because the young man is an active sentry rather than one of those that sits and waits out his shift. I don't envy Roy, and his young wife Peg, who ride just behind Galusha Gains and Samuel Grosvenor, especially knowing what those men think of the color of Roy's skin.

Well after dark, while making my rounds, I surprise the stranger where he stands relieving himself.

I turn my back and clear my throat and wait until he's finished. "Forgive the intrusion, Mister. My name is Dorcas."

"What the blazes are you doing sneaking around in the dark, this time of night. You trying to get yourself killed?"

"I'm on patrol, standing watch. What's your name, friend?"

"I'm Dell. Delbert, if you must know. Boss Wheel lets women stand guard nowadays?"

"Not women, Mr. Dell. Just me. I'm handy with rifles and pistols. He says I'll do."

Our visitor lets off what sounds like a week's worth of accumulated, excess gas. "Pardon my enthusiasm, lady. Dang beans chew up my gut." The veteran mountain man turns away and disappears, without parting pleasantries and I continue to make my way around the circled wagons' outer perimeter. I'd like to say all is quiet, but the sound of retching can be heard at several points along the way.

If this heat spell doesn't break soon, somebody's going to perish. Maybe we'll all be baked alive in the Devil's furnace.

THURSDAY, AUGUST 15

IN THE MORNING, I try not to rub my eyes for fear of pressing abrasive dust into them. It would be heavenly to wash my face, but water isn't to be wasted on such a luxury. It doesn't feel as if sleep was accompanied by restfulness, but morning has come, nevertheless. As the dipper draws a cup of salvation from the barrel, I watch our visitor ride off toward the east, carrying his troublesome news with him. I drink slowly, imagining the fluid is a quenching nectar instead of sand flavored water.

I pass the ladle to Andrew. "Another hot one?"

"Yes, Mama. It isn't going to break today."

"Heaven help us, son."

"I wish I had better news."

"Me too. Hope we can find fresh water today."

Andrew rises to the tips of his toes and looks into the barrel. "Me too, Mama. We're two thirds down."

"I know."

Christopher, Dahlia Jane, and Stillman are lined up behind Andrew. To no one in particular, I say, "We better try not to waste a single drop." It's hard to think we're so close to a major river, yet we struggle to find water.

When we stop for our dinner break at midday, there's no water at our picnic spot. Lunch is a hunk of dried, jerked meat, a dry biscuit, and a cup of gritty water. There's a dint of intrigue to the south, where it appears there are barren mountains, but our route lies in a northwesterly direction. The urge to crawl beneath the wagon and refuse to budge is strong, but we obediently resume our slow hot march when the bugle sounds.

Despite the heat, when we reach the end of the day, a jubilant cheer travels from wagon to wagon at the sight of a line of trees. It is as if we've been hopelessly lost at sea and suddenly catch sight of land on the horizon. A line of trees often means a river, stream, or creek lies ahead. Hopefully there's water. In any case, we'll have shade and firewood. Though it's too hot to imagine wanting a fire, we'll want to collect some in case it is scarce ahead. But collecting firewood is a chore and all we want to do is get away from the sun and collapse.

When the wagons circle up and the chores are done, everyone wanders off and I'm left with Dahlia Jane. I grab a bucket and make my way to Rock Creek. It would seem there are more rocks than water in the meager trickle during the mid-August drought, but there is enough to dip a bucket into. As we begin to make our way back to the wagon, a bright yellow flower catches my eye. "Oh, my goodness. Dahlia Jane! It's a sunflower."

The child jumps up and down for joy. Who else has the energy to leap into the air and cheer? It seems like ages since anybody has shown such glee.

"Have you ever eaten a sunflower seed, dear?"

"You can eat them?"

"No, not the flower, but there are seeds inside. You'll see. Let's get a bag and collect them."

News of our find travels fast, and soon everyone is harvesting the bright flowers. I think of the birds that depend on the seeds to get through the winter. Hopefully, there are plenty elsewhere because we've not left any at the edge of Rock Creek. I wonder how many wagon trains have passed by without realizing the bounty within their reach.

When we return to camp with sacks full of sunflower heads, I see Gwibunzi standing behind a wagon with her head in the opening. What has happened? This can't be good. Whose wagon is that?

Just my luck, of all the wagons to poke her head into, Gwibunzi had to pick Captain Meadows' prairie schooner. My heart drops as I reach for her halter and whisper soothing words into her ear, just as Captain Meadows appears around the wagon's corner.

"What is going on, Mrs. Moon? I thought I told you to keep that misfit away from the wagons."

"I'm sorry. It seems she has escaped. I'll take her back to the picket line."

As I lead the mustang back toward the picket line, Captain Meadows shouts after me. "Come back here at once, Mrs. Moon."

I turn around and start back toward the preacher's wagon. "Not now. After you get rid of that nag."

My voice reassures Gwibunzi. "Don't listen to him. You're no such thing." As I lead her back to the picket line, I realize that the rope is not frayed, but rather, the break in the rope has been sliced cleanly. Someone cut her loose. Who could have done such a thing? Are they out to get me or frame the horse?

I find another lead rope and quickly tie the mustang to the picket line. My hands clutch the evidence as my feet hurry back to Captain Meadows' wagon.

The mayor of our rolling village is consumed with rage and brays like a donkey. He doesn't seem to care about the severed lead rope. Instead, he wants me to see the overturned keg of oats, which is practically empty. "I want you to free that wild animal. She will never be tamed."

"But Captain Meadows, any horse would steal oats if it had the chance. She could have run away and returned to the wilderness. Instead, she came here."

The furious man shakes as he screams. "I don't want to hear another word."

"I'll make it up to you, sir. I don't know how many oats I have left, but you can have whatever remains in our barrel."

Luella appears beside her husband, grips his elbow, and says, "That sounds fair, Mortimer."

The irate preacher grumbles and bows his head. I wink at Mrs. Meadows, conspiratorially, and with a quick nod, I turn and hurry away. Hopefully, the man will forget the incident. What will I do if he banishes Gwibunzi? I don't know if I could part with the mare now.

FRIDAY, AUGUST 16

IN THE MORNING, ROSE appears in camp and I wonder what her husband has planned for the day. Rose fills our ears with a fantastic story about camping beside a towering pair of waterfalls a couple of miles away. While we parked beside a trickle of a tributary, Rose and Snarling Wolf bathed in the mist of a roaring cataract. She looks fresh as a spring flower, whereas the rest of us look like mud-caked zombies.

Dahlia Jane interrupts. "We found sunflowers. Show her, Mama."

Rose looks curiously into a sack and I place a few green seeds in the palm of her hand. "They'll be better when they dry, especially if we can spare a shake or two of salt." The back of our wagon is practically overloaded with sacks of flowerheads.

Andrew holds out his hand for some sunflower seeds.

As I fill his palm, I ask, "Any rain today, dear?"

"No, afraid not. Sunny, hot, and no rain."

"At least the water barrel is full."

The trumpet blasts just as I finish telling Rose about Gwibunzi's adventure and the depletion of Captain Meadows' keg of oats. It's time to move. Rose doesn't seem to care about the mustang anyway.

As the wagon begins to roll, I say to Christopher, "What day is this, anyway? I've lost track."

"It's Friday, Mama. Can you believe it?"

"It is hard to keep track of what day it is, especially when the weather never seems to change."

"When can I dump the sling, Mama?"

My brain tries to calculate an answer. "Good Heavens, dear. What day is it now?"

"Oh Mama, today is the sixteenth."

I frown. "I'm sorry, Christopher. You still have a couple of weeks left to go. I'm sorry."

He grumbles, scoffs, mumbles unintelligible words, and begins to whine. It isn't like him to complain. "I feel like a prisoner. This blame arm makes me useless. I don't want to wear this contraption anymore."

"I know my love."

Christopher kicks the ground and cracks the whip in the air. "I'm tired of spending all day talking to the butt end of an ox."

I want to laugh at my nine-year-old son's way with words, but I manage to contain my amusement. "I know it is exhausting, but you've done the work of almost two men. I'm very proud of you, dear. I'm going to have to give you a big old hug and kiss."

Christopher's head lifts and I can see the proud look on his face even under the thick coat of ash-colored dust on his skin. "No, Mama. Not that. I'll stop complaining. I promise." There's a playful look in his eyes as we begin our day on the trail.

At the other end of the day, we cross the creek we've been following all day. After walking with our oxen all morning, Christopher spent the afternoon driving Minor Shaw's wagon. At midday, the old shipbuilder announced that he would go no farther, but Agapito brokered a deal to keep his wagon moving. At supper, Christopher says, "I spent all day listening to that old man tell pirate stories, but at least I have two dimes to show for it. He says if I come back tomorrow, he'll let me trade the two dimes for a half dollar.

Andrew gripes at Christopher. "Don't think I'm going to do your share here while you get rich over there."

"Yeah, yeah. Listen to you. I walk with our oxen more than you ever do."

The boy's disagreement continues far too long. I'm not sure who is technically correct. In this heat, I don't know how they find the energy to muster a spirited disagreement. I don't even have enough to adjudicate their dispute. They shall have to work it out. When Snarling Wolf appears at the edge of camp, I barely have enough energy to lift my arm in distant greeting as Rose scampers away.

During a lull in Christopher's argument with Andrew, Christopher says, "Mr. Shaw says he saw Mr. Gains with a knife and was afraid the man was going to stab Gwibunzi. He was relieved to see that Mr. Gains just cut the rope."

It was just as I suspected. I figured it was possible that Samuel Grosvenor or Horace Blocker cut the line, but Galusha Gains was always my lead suspect. What good does knowing do anyway? What can I do about the situation now?

I tell Christopher to try and make sure that Minor Shaw stays in the shade, drinks a lot of water, and takes it easy.

"Yes, Mama. Mostly, Mrs. Shaw looks after him. But he complains. He says she pesters him too much."

As the sun edges over the horizon, Agapito wanders over. "Is everything good?"

I shrug. "Suppose so."

"I thought I heard an argument."

"The boys had a few cross words earlier. It seems to have passed."

Seemingly out of the blue, Agapito asks, "Are you missing Lucky Nye?"

"Dearie me, Agapito. I haven't thought about him in days." Why is Agapito asking me about Lucky Nye?

"Oh. I thought it would take you a while to get over him."

"Get over him?"

"Yes. You were close, no?"

"Close friends, I guess. Why do you mention it?" My cheeks warm recalling our passionate embrace, and the other man who I pictured when I closed my eyes.

Agapito turns slightly away from me. "I could not help seeing you in his arms. It looked like you were more than friendly."

"Oh, I see. There really wasn't much to it. He is a good-looking man. I don't know what came over him, but when he wrapped his arms around me and kissed me, I got swept away, lost in the moment, and thought I was somewhere else. I do miss Lucky, but I do not pine for him. He warms my heart, Agapito, but my heart doesn't burn for him. Do you understand?"

Agapito turns back and faces me. "Of course, *estimada*. Lucky is a good man and so is his son."

How long has it been since he has called me that? Could he have been jealous? What a preposterous thought.

SATURDAY, AUGUST 17

SATURDAY AFTERNOON, WE SET camp a little bit earlier than usual. As the scouts set up their camp, I walk over.

Arikta and Dembi Koofai work together to stake the canvas awning. Boss Wheel and Agapito are having a conversation. Usually, Boss Wheel becomes silent whenever I am present, but today he doesn't seem to care that I am here. "The heat has cooked the loco out of our greenhorns. It's Saturday night and the droopy pilgrims don't have enough energy to cause trouble anymore." Old Wagon Wheel seems pleased.

Agapito says, "Should we plan a dance?"

Boss Wheel shakes his head. "Too hot for that. They'll collapse, *certainement*. It is a good thing we have the heat to distract them from the crazy."

Agapito turns to me and says, "Every year, it is the same. When we get to the Snake River, everybody turns loco."

Almost on cue, loud voices near The Hub pull our attention from our conversation. The situation reminds me of the day in Independence, just before our journey commenced. We hurry to the center of the circle.

Bobby says, "Your sister is as ugly as you are."

Wayne shouts, "What did you marry her for then?"

Bobby gripes, "You poisoned every other girl in town, so you could have them all to yourself. Then, you had to go and marry my sister."

Wayne accuses, "Never mind Drucilla. You married my sister just to get back at me, didn't you?"

Bobby grouses, "Your mother's ugly too." He spits into the dirt. "I see where you and your sister get your looks from."

Wayne jumps forward, thrusts his fists into Bobby's chest and topples him into the thick dust. "It makes me sick to think that my father gave you $500. He didn't give me a blame thing. Half that money should have been mine. Don't you think your sister deserves half of that money? Think about Drucilla's baby."

Bobby jumps to his feet and throws a blue arm in Wayne's direction, landing a fist on his jaw. "You mean Floyd and Drucilla's baby?"

Wayne kicks Bobby in the gut, doubling him over and knocking the breath from him. "Take that back. Floyd and Drucilla broke off their engagement a year ago."

On all fours, while trying to catch his breath, Bobby says, "Drucilla would still rather have your brother than you."

Wayne pounces onto Bobby's back and they tumble about in the thick, chalky dust. Before long, it is hard to tell one man from the other, as the red shirt and blue, both become dirt gray.

Once again, nobody does anything. I don't have the energy to play marshal today, but if I don't do it, who will? I shout, "Don't make me come over there." There's no indication that they can hear me. Why must we do this, over and over again?

Flailing arms knock into me as I pluck one, and then the other, from the ground and strong arm them beyond each other's reach. Their mouths hang open as they see their pregnant wives approaching. Drucilla carries two bottles of whiskey and Serena holds a third. The men whimper in unison as Drucilla and Serena turn the whiskey bottles upside down.

The young man to my right squeaks, "Oh, no, honey, that's all we have left. Please don't do that."

To my left, I hear, "Stop, before it's too late. Before it's all gone. Unhand me, Dorcas." He begs, pitifully. "Please?"

The men sag as the last of their whiskey glugs to the ground. I'm too weak to hold their dead weight any longer. I release one and then the other, and drop them back to the ground. They slowly climb to their feet and follow their wives back to their wagons, like dogs with their tails between their legs.

Agapito appears beside me. "It is hard to imagine they can stand each other at all. Do you think it is just the whiskey talking? Those two always seem like best friends, but it sounds like they have just as much reason to be enemies."

I say, "It seems they are quick to forgive, even if they can't forget. Could you imagine if your best friend was also your worst enemy?"

Agapito flashes a playful grin and says, "Let us hope their wives are as quick to forgive as they are, *estimada*."

I tip my head as if looking to God for assistance. "They're just like a couple of children. Those boys shouldn't be married, marching across the desert. Soon, they will be fathers and have children of their own. They're practically children themselves. Heaven help them."

Agapito bends his arm and gallantly leads me back to my wagon. When we arrive, Christopher and Andrew are bickering again. I think of the hot-heads from Pennsylvania. My boys had better not start throwing punches. I imagine myself jumping into the fray and separating Andrew and Christopher. Andrew is older, but I'd bet on Christopher. He's scrappy enough, but then I remember his arm is in a sling. Though they're years younger than Bobby and Wayne, in some ways, they're far more mature than the expectant fathers.

Christopher says, "You don't even care about Father's watch. You only want it because I do."

Andrew answers, "I'm the oldest, so I should get Father's watch. A news-paperman needs a watch."

Christopher laughs, as if to add to his insults. "You're not a newspaperman. You need a printing press to be a newspaperman."

I must agree with Christopher about Larkin's watch. He was the one who insisted on fixing the timepiece at Fort Hall. Does Andrew only want it because Christopher wishes to have it? In any case, what does it matter now? "Alright men, stop arguing. Father's watch belongs to me now, so let's not discuss it anymore."

Agapito says something quickly in Spanish. The only word I comprehend is *loco*.

Andrew and Christopher head in different directions and Agapito makes his way back to his own wagon. A few minutes later, I hear the sound of a fiddle wailing. It isn't the usual, jubilant square dancing music we've come to expect on Saturday nights, but rather, a beautiful, but haunting melody.

Bobby and Wayne may be quick to forget, but it isn't the same with Christopher and Andrew. The second that breakfast is over and the chores are done, Christopher disappears and Andrew relaxes.

I inquire, "Any rain today?"

"No, Mama. More of the same, but not for too much longer. I think we will have another day or two of heat."

I sigh. If he's correct, I should be glad that the end of the heat spell is on the way.

Andrew's face twists in confusion. "Something's going to happen today, Mama. I don't know if it will be good or bad, but something is definitely going to happen."

Stillman arrives with an armload of firewood as Christopher races back into camp. "Honey's having her puppies. Come quick."

Andrew follows his brother to Alvah's camp and Stillman trails behind them.

Dahlia Jane grabs her doll by the hair and says, "Why can't Honey have kittens instead of puppies?"

"I guess it doesn't work that way, dear." The child makes her way over to Cobb's wagon to play with Bess and Joe, and my attention turns to baking and washing. Despite my disdain for the washboard, I do enjoy changing into clean clothes every once in a while. With Rose gone, nobody else is going to launder our clothing.

Though I've invited Rose to bring her husband to dinner, I fret about what to serve. We've grown so weary of pancakes, bacon, and beans. The last of our eggs barely binds a sorry looking cake flavored with the last drops of peppermint extract. At noon, I wonder how long it takes a dog to have a litter of puppies. The wash is done and hung, the cake is stowed away in the wagon, and the last of the biscuits are browning up. We could use more firewood and I could get some water.

Before I can decide what to do next, Snarling Wolf appears carrying a quarter of an antelope. He drops it by the campfire with a grunt and a nod.

I'm grateful to have meat and start to thank him as Christopher races into camp, followed by Andrew and Stillman. "Look, Mama." He holds his hands out and I'm surprised to see a tiny version of Honey. Of course, I knew they wouldn't be very big, but I wasn't expecting them to be as small as this. "This one didn't make it, Mama." He pets the little dog with his finger.

Snarling Wolf says, "Could I have it?"

Christopher hands him the dead puppy.

"Thank you. It is a delicacy." Snarling Wolf spins on his heel and vanishes around the corner of the wagon.

Christopher looks at me with a shocked look on his face. "I thought he just wanted to look at it. Do you really think he's going to eat him? I was going to bury the puppy."

"I'm sorry, dear. I don't know. Maybe it is best not to think about it. Were there other puppies?"

Breathlessly, Christopher answers. "Yes, Mama. There are four. Alvah says I can have first choice."

I gasp. I can't help myself. There's not much that scares me, but there's not much difference between wolves and dogs, to my way of thinking. I knew Christopher hoped to have a puppy, but now that they've been born, it's hard to put off the inevitability of one joining the family. Learning to appreciate Honey took time and effort. Now, I don't even mind the Irish Setter, Chestnut, though he's too unpredictable for my taste.

"It will be alright, Mama. You'll see. Why, I bet you'll fall in love with the puppy too. How will I choose just one?"

My official consent has not yet been given, though I fully understand it would crush Christopher's heart if I were to object now. "How long do the puppies stay with Honey?"

"About two months, I think. They should be ready about the same time we get to Oregon, Mama."

Andrew says, "Told you something would happen today, Mama."

It's as hot as ever, but suddenly the wind picks up. Dust fills the air and I squint to block it from my eyes. There are still chores to tend to. "Who wants to help me with the butchering?"

Nobody volunteers, so Stillman steps forward, hefts the carcass and heads for the river. "I'll take care of it."

"I'll slow cook it into stew when you get back."

He raises an eyebrow. "You won't even need a fire to do it. Just set it in a pot and it'll cook itself."

Christopher and Andrew recommence their argument over Larkin's pocket watch. Andrew makes the point that Christopher gets a puppy, so to be fair, Andrew should get the watch. Christopher doesn't think one thing has anything to do with the other and goes on to proclaim, "You always get everything you want, just because you're the oldest. I gotta work for everything I get. Might as well go live with Alvah Nye."

Andrew says, "You practically already do."

To halt the argument, I say, "I've been thinking about our home in Oregon." Dahlia Jane makes her way to the campfire, climbs into my lap, and wraps her arms around me. It's too hot for close contact, but I'm not going to push her away. "What do we know about building log cabins? If we arrive in October, it will practically be winter already. Do you think we can do it?"

Christopher says, "I'll have my arm back by then."

Andrew asks, "Will we each have a bed of our own?"

"I don't know. We'll probably have to start with a very small home at first and add on to it next year."

Dahlia Jane asks, "Who will live with us?"

Christopher scoffs, "Who do you think?"

Dahlia Jane begins to make a list. "Mama, Andrew, Christopher, Me, my dolly, Stillman, Alvah, Agapito, Bess, Joe, Cobb, Rick Taw, Debbie Coffee, Old Wheel, and Honey."

Christopher rolls his eyes.

Andrew says, "If all those people are going to live with us, they can build the cabin."

"Do you think you could sketch out a place big enough for five of us, Andrew? We'd better practice with the axe as much as possible. I'm not sure if anyone will be able to help us when we get there." I can't help but notice that Dahlia Jane left Rose and Snarling Wolf off her long list. A salty tear threatens to spill from my eye, but I blink it away. She's probably right. Most likely, my oldest child will winter elsewhere. I can only hope they'll stay in Oregon at least until spring.

A tumbleweed bowls its way between wagons, careens across the diameter, and crashes into the side of our wagon before the wind sucks it beneath our wagon and expels it from the encampment.

MONDAY, AUGUST 19

WHEN WE MAKE CAMP, late Monday afternoon, Cian Reid makes his way around the wagon circle. As he passes by, he tips his head back as if trying to catch the scent of our supper. Is it my imagination, or can I see his nose wiggling as he sniffs? "What's that you have simmering in the pot there?" he asks.

"Just bacon and beans, I'm afraid." I glance about to see if Oona is anywhere nearby. "Would you care to join us, Cian?"

He says that he can only stay a short while, shovels food into his mouth, and scrapes the tin plate clean. The lustful look on his face makes it seem like he might lick the plate clean. Sometimes, I've noticed, he eats like he's afraid that someone will take his food away from him. Other times, he tries to make his food last, so that he'll always have something to eat.

I ask, "Would you like a biscuit?"

A wide expression crosses his face and he stands taller. Optimistically, he says, "Sounds fine. Sure enough." He examines it closely and takes a small taste as if testing it to make sure it isn't poisonous. I remember when I first met Cian and Oona, how he nibbled on a roll with a cross emblazoned on top. How long can he make my unblessed biscuit last?

Before Cian departs, Agapito blows his trumpet at The Hub, summoning us to a rare gathering. Boss Wheel stands beside his assistant, nodding agreement as Agapito speaks. We are warned about the Indians that we are likely to encounter in the coming weeks. "Most will keep their distance. This time of year, we will see many in the river. They harvest salmon from the current and dry the fish to last throughout the winter. Do not shoot at the Indians." Agapito turns as he speaks, making eye contact with our most hotheaded travelers. "Do not threaten them. Do not taunt them. Do not even try to speak with them. Leave it to us. This is why you hired us instead of the other guides. Avoid looking directly at them. If they want to trade with us, we will let you know, and we will gather here to trade." He points to the post that houses *The Rolling Home Times* as if it were symbolic of our circular village square. "*¿Comprende?*"

Wandering away, I overhear Cian ask Oona, "Sorry, what is salmon?"

She shrugs. "Some kind of fish. Isn't that what he said?"

How did he miss that part? Cian says to Oona, "Sounds grand. We can have a feast. We be running low on food, me dear lady."

Oona hands baby Aengus to him, straightens her bright strawberry blond hair, and asks if he can fill the water barrel while she does some baking. An image of Cobb carrying baby Jenny in one arm and a bucket in the other appears in my head as the Irishman carries his son toward the river. Then, I imagine him leaving the baby beside the river to chase after salmon. Would it be possible for us to catch fish, as do the Indians?

Christopher tugs at my sleeve and says, "Come see the river, Mama."

After a short trek, we look out over the edge of a hillside, not nearly as steep as the cliff at Cauldron Linn. The Snake River's frothy rapids are impressive, and one might imagine the dramatic plumes when the water levels flood in the spring.

I feel a touch of a headache. Why did we make an unnecessary hike after walking all day?

The cheerful rapids lifted my spirits for a brief moment and then were quickly forgotten. It's a dry and sweaty day. The urge to swallow is strong, though my mouth is parched. It seems like forever since we enjoyed a cool breeze. The hot sandy wind we experienced yesterday did nothing to refresh us. The only thing that keeps my brain from cooking in my head is Andrew's prediction that the heat spell will soon end.

The dizziness that accompanied my fever and ague returns like a bad memory, and all I want to do is return to the wagon and retire for the evening. Christopher tugs at my sleeve and says, "Let's go see the puppies, Mama. C'mon. You promised." He's done nothing but talk about the newborn litter all day. The urge to wave him off and let him go alone is strong, but I think of the look on Andrew's face whenever I'm forced to admit that I haven't read the news of the day. I yawn, stretch my shoulders, and tell Christopher that we can go, as my hand reaches for the dipper.

Before the water touches my lips, my legs give way beneath me. My last recollection is of closing my eyes and seeing an endless sea of sandy brown, like the dreary landscape we've been traveling through, and a feeling of falling. A shock of water splashes my face in my next lucid moment as I blink moisture away from my eyes. With a gag, I roll to my knees and begin to hork, only nothing comes when I arch my back and retch onto the soil.

I hear Christopher's desperate voice. "Will Mama be okay?"

A man's hands grip my shoulders. "I am here, *estimada*. Try to breathe. Tell yourself not to vomit. We need to cool you down."

The involuntary spasms force me to retch again. The man beside me gathers my hair and I wish that I could disappear. When I have dreamed of him running his hands through my hair, it didn't look anything like this.

Agapito says, "You are not with child, are you?"

My convulsions give way to a fit of coughing. I turn from kneeling and stretch out on my back. My hair drags through the dusty sand. As the coughing wanes, I gasp. "Good Heavens, no. That would be impossible. How could you think such a thing?" As the words trickle from my lips, my mind goes blank again.

TUESDAY, AUGUST 20

IT'S DARK, THOUGH MY eyes are open. What happened? Where am I? With a shiver and a realization that hours have passed, the familiarity of my surroundings dawns in my head, accompanied by an awareness that something isn't normal. The sound of Dahlia Jane, like a purring kitten fast asleep beside me, is reassuring. I blink as my vision makes out the form of a man in the wagon with us. We are not alone.

I turn my head. The dim form of a silhouette is hard to identify. The words begin to form on my lips as the soothing voice inquires.

"You are feeling better, yes?"

My voice sounds gravelly to my own ears. "I think so. Have you been here all night? Am I dying?"

"Yes, I have been here. No, you are not dying. I will not allow it."

When I sit up, clammy rags fall from my wrists. My teeth chatter as my arms circle my knees. For the first time in ages, I'm cold. "Has the heat spell broken?"

"A cool breeze kicked up about midnight. That is when your fever broke. You drank a good amount of water and went back to sleep. You have forgotten that. You should drink again, *estimada*."

Agapito takes my hand in his and wraps my fingers around a tumbler.

"*¡Beber!*"

After a couple of tentative sips, I drink deeply and almost empty the container.

An approving grunt is followed by a gentle command. "More. You will need to drink a lot of water today."

When the vessel is empty, my hands meet Agapito's again and he takes the tumbler from me. "Today? Is it morning then?"

"*Sí*, it is time to roust the pilgrims from their slumber. Will you ride in the wagon today?"

After a brief negotiation, I convince the assistant wagon master that I am strong enough to ride Blizzard and if I feel weak, I will climb aboard. He pauses before leaping from the back of the wagon as if he is afraid of falling from the edge of a cliff. Finally, he says, "I am glad you are feeling better." Why were those words hard for him to come by? A half second later, his feet thud onto the ground behind the wagon and, as I lower my feet to the ground, the familiar honk of the trumpet breaks the silence. I close my eyes and picture his lips on the mouthpiece as his slender fingers plunge the valves.

The brothers draw a pair of wagons from the end of a long, slow-moving wagon train. Between the two rigs, there are half a dozen, beautiful young women in addition to the middle-aged parents that accompany them.

The Radish begs The Viper to let the girls go.

"What's the matter with you? You used to just ask if you could keep one. Now you want to save them? All of them?"

"Why not? They're just girls."

"Just girls? Haven't you listened to a thing I've said?" The Viper shoves his brother to the ground and swiftly slays the girls' parents while Sloan threatens to shoot the screaming girls. When the parents are dead, The Viper's slashing blade drops the young girls, quickly, one after the other, from loudest to m eekest.

It crosses The Viper's mind that he should make The Radish kill the last one. It's way past time for him to draw first blood. Soon, he tells himself. Next time, maybe.

The Radish stands, frozen. His hardened eyes have witnessed such horrors throughout the years. Usually, The Viper does his worst from farther away. It's bad enough to know that his brothers kill people, but it's another thing to witness it close up. How can he just stand by and let it happen? He must admit it saddens him when The Viper kills ugly old people. Though he's never been taught or shown otherwise, somehow, he knows it's wrong, tragic even. Why must they kill such pretty young ladies? What a waste.

When the family has settled in for the evening after a fifteen mile trek, I take a deep drink though I'm not thirsty, just to placate my worried family. I saddle up for a brief ride. Movement in the wagon master's camp catches my eye. Boss Wheel knees Clipper in the ribs to expel air from the horse's lungs before tightening the cinch strap around the girth.

I climb into the saddle and follow a small group of fellow travelers toward the river. The clip clop sound of horses' hooves lets me know that I am not alone. A flutter of excitement tickles my belly as I remember riding off to see Scotts Bluff with Agapito, ages ago now. I close my eyes and picture the handsome man sitting high in the saddle, with his legs astride his golden steed. That man spent the night beside my bed. Mere hours ago, his hands enveloped mine as he nursed me back to health. I sigh, glance over my shoulder, and I am surprised to see Boss Wheel. Somehow, I had forgotten that he followed me from camp rather than Agapito.

When Blizzard reaches the river, he bends his stocky, silver-whorled neck and drinks deeply. Boss Wheel appears beside me and Clipper dips his muzzle into the Snake River. The reticent trail boss dips his hands into one of the pockets of his capote and extracts his field glass. He passes them to me and says, "Look there."

It takes me a while to adjust the focus and find the target. Boss Wheel rolls a crude smoke and clears his throat while I close one eye and squint through the other. When I gasp, the mountain man chuckles. "Found it, didn't you?"

"Oh, Mr. Roulette. It's a wonder. What is this place called?"

"Thousand Springs." He strikes a friction match, lights his smoke, moistens his thumb and forefinger with his tongue, and pinches the end of the match cold before flipping it into the river. "Let's ride over and get a closer look." Without waiting to see if I agree to accompany him, Boss Wheel presses his boot heel into Clipper's belly and splashes across the shallow river. When we reach the other side, Boss Wheel sits back in the saddle and gazes at the mossy emerald oasis. An elegant veil of pure white covers the rocky wall, contrasting brilliantly with the colors of the vibrant plant life.

With gushing optimism that I can't contain, I exclaim, "It's a sublime spectacle."

"That's a good way to put it. She is my favorite place on earth. Most people never get to see such a sight. You and I, Mrs. Moon, we are the lucky ones. A sublime spectacle, you say. I never feel more alive than when I am here. If it weren't for this place, I don't know whether I'd bother making this trip every year. We are lucky to be alive, are we not?"

Though I wish Agapito were my chaperone today, I'm glad to share such a pleasant moment with the hardened mountain man. I burp and taste acid in the back of my throat and feel like vomit will follow. Now that the heat has faded, I expect I'll be fine. I reach for my carried water and drink deeply, while I burn the sight of a thousand cascades into my memory.

Wednesday, August 21

FOR THE SECOND DAY in a row, I awaken with a shiver. It's still August, the peak of summer, and yet the cool morning air whispers like the chill of an early autumn.

We were promised a long march today, a voyage of some 22 miles, and warned to fill the barrels in advance of a dry camp in the middle of nowhere, as if we haven't been in the middle of nowhere for many months now. Even after all this time in the wilderness, the thrill of the unknown still captivates me. But this freedom has come at such a high price. With chores to do, such thoughts are banished from my mind, or perhaps saved for later. There will be time to ruminate on them during our daily march.

Christopher bursts into camp and breathlessly informs us that one of Honey's puppies has perished overnight. The blind baby dog wiggled off in the wrong direction, failed to find its way back to its littermates, and froze to death a couple of feet from its family. My son's lower lip shows how he feels, but his firm eyebrows show his determination not to cry. "Honey's still got three pups left, Mama. You still haven't seen 'em, have you? You gotta let me show you."

I promise to go with Christopher after we set out for the day.

Andrew says, "You're not going to spend all day over there again today, are you?"

His brother says, "Maybe I will. What's it to you?"

"Why should I spend all day walking with the oxen? You need to do your fair share, Christopher."

I scratch my chin. Perhaps I've been lucky all these years. My sons never argued much, as do other mothers' sons. But, after growing up listening to Larkin and me, it is a wonder they don't bicker all the time. This isn't the first time I've noticed them. When did their relationship begin to deteriorate? That's something else to ponder. I would agree with Andrew, but Christopher is only nine. Despite his lack of years, Christopher is stronger and harder working than most boys several years older. Andrew is lucky to have had somebody to split the chores with. If it weren't for Christopher, Andrew, and Stillman, I would have to spend all day, every day, marching alongside. Though I would like to intervene, and release Christopher, I decide to let the boys work it out as Larkin would advise.

Christopher argues, "My fair share? Half the time I walk all day while you make newspapers nobody reads." I wince, feeling guilty for not reading yet another issue of *The Rolling Home Times*, and at the same time wishing I had stopped the disagreement before such words were spoken.

"Take that back."

"No, Andrew. I won't. Alvah pays me to work for him and he's nice. You make me do all your work and you don't even thank me. Alvah acts more like a brother than you do."

"Gosh, Christopher. I don't know what you're talking about. I spend so much time plodding along, I feel like I'm strapped in with the oxen and my fingers feel like they're frozen to the whip handle."

I intervene, "Alright boys. I think, if we're honest, Stillman tends the oxen more than the rest of us put together. What if we divide the days into shifts?"

They grumble and then return to a familiar argument. Christopher says, "Who is going to keep track of time?" The boys argue about who should be the keeper of Larkin's watch. I knew I shouldn't have intervened.

I had planned to keep the time piece for the time being, if only to avoid being accused of favoring one son over the other. I say, "I'll do my best to let everyone know when it is their turn." We split the day in quarters, starting with Christopher, then me, then Andrew after dinner, and Stillman will finish each day. Truth be told, Stillman spends most of his time on one side of the oxen or the other.

For the first couple of hours, the trail parallels the Snake River. As the sun rises, we begin seeing Indians in the river. It's hard to do as instructed. I can't help watching them. It looks like their hands and the water they fish in, are bloody, but it's the masses of bright red fish that make it seem so. Mostly, the busy Indians ignore us, but occasionally, they look in our direction. Are they curious about us, or do they wish we'd just disappear? It's hard not to feel like trespassers and interlopers. Intruding on them is yet another thing to feel guilty about. I wonder whether we will displace other Indians when we build our cabin, when we reach our destination.

Midmorning, Christopher's shift ends, and he disappears. It's my turn to lead the team as the trail diverges from the river and we trudge into the vast desert. After our midday dinner break, I leave Dahlia Jane and the wagon to Andrew and Stillman, and make my way to Alvah's wagon.

After a pleasant greeting, the young man says, "You must be here to see the pups."

The expression on my face betrays my attempt to conceal my thoughts.

"Don't worry, Dorcas. I can assure you, you have nothing to be afraid of. We've had lots of curiosity seekers and Honey doesn't object to having visitors."

With a determined nod and a quick step, my feet take me to the back of the bachelor's prairie schooner. Christopher's back is propped against the back of the wagon. Honey is sprawled out with her head on his lap and three tiny puppies are latched on. Christopher's broken arm is draped over Honey's back and his other hand strokes the retriever's chest.

As if trying to avoid waking the dog, Christopher whispers loudly. "Oh, Mama. You came. What do you think? Did you ever see anything like them?"

"Yes. And yet, the miracle of new life never fails to melt my heart." What was I afraid of? Neither the oblivious adult nor the wriggling whelplings look anything like the wolves in my nightmares.

"Would you like to hold one?"

"I'm not sure, Christopher. I'd hate to disturb them. They look a bit busy at the moment."

With his good arm, he plucks one from a teat and thrusts it toward me. "It's okay. They don't mind," he says, as if he could know their thoughts.

"I think that one's my favorite. I think she looks the most like her mother. What do you think?"

"I guess the others have a little bit of a redder color, and wavy fur." I should warn him not to become too attached in case something happens, but it's too late. There's no love more pure than what resides in the heart of a nine-year-old boy, and often, dogs are the beneficiaries of those most tender emotions. "What's Alvah going to do with the other puppies?"

"He doesn't know. Everybody wants one. He asked me to make a list of anybody who is interested, but not to make any promises, except of course, he has promised me I could have first choice."

The puppy in my hand begins to squirm and I pass it back to Christopher. "Have you got a name picked out?" Dahlia Jane's doll comes to mind. I suppose naming a dog is different from naming a pretend baby.

"Alvah says not to worry about that. Her name will come to me and when I hear it, I'll know it."

Though it seems an odd thing to say, I thank Christopher for inviting me to come and see Honey's puppies.

I spend a couple of minutes with Alvah before returning to our wagon. Over the past two weeks, we haven't had much time together and I'm curious whether he misses his father. He says, "I still can't get over the shock of having a father since I never did. It made me realize, there is so much I want to see and do. I'm not meant to turn the soil or stay in one place. What ever made me think of going to Oregon to become a farmer? Maybe I'll make my way by hunting and trapping. I have discovered that I have a restless spirit."

"I've never known anybody who had a more settled soul, but perhaps you do have a restless spirit." Sometimes the idiotic things that come from my mouth amaze me. Aren't spirits and souls the same thing? Strangely, Alvah doesn't offer an argument to my suggestion.

On my way back to the wagon, the young man's future is on my mind. He doesn't want to be a farmer, yet he plans to complete the journey to Oregon. He says he might make a living as a hunter or trapper. Ultimately, what will he decide to do with his life?

THURSDAY, AUGUST 22

WE ARE SUPPOSED TO complete a 23-mile trek today. Those with mules are impatient with our oxen propelled wagons, but the day threatens to expire before we reunite with the Snake River, and finally, the lead wagon loops into a circle. For the second day in a row, we must endure a dry camp.

As we work on end of day chores, Andrew and Christopher bicker about their future professions. Every job has its merits and all work contributes to the common need. Why should Christopher care if Andrew wants to be a newspaperman? What's it to Andrew if Christopher endeavors to become a soldier? The only one who doesn't say anything about his aspirations is Stillman. What will become of Stillman?

There's nothing combustible and I worry about running out of firewood. It's been ages since we've seen buffalo chips. On the remote chance that I might find something for a campfire, I saddle up and quickly ride off to the northwest, not straying far from the trail's ruts. Encountering some scrubby sage I prepare my lasso, thinking that I might find a dead cottonwood or a big shrub to drag back to camp.

Soon, it will be dark, and I'm about to turn around and return when, to my right, I see a small herd of wild horses in a draw. Remembering how Dembi Koofai suggested wandering slowly into the herd, I do my best to relax my overexcited heartbeat. I gently loosen my hold on the reins and let Blizzard step forward at will. I coo reassuring sentiments, hoping that my horse understands what I want rather than the emotion I'm trying to cover up. An anxious mare snorts and her ears flicker. Near me, an inquisitive mare bends her neck in my direction. Blizzard nickers at her and the red roan approaches. She seems to be as curious about my cooing noises as she is in Blizzard's vocalizations. The wild horse doesn't object in the slightest when I gently place my rope over her head. She follows us willingly and easily as we step back toward the southeast.

As we make our way back toward the wagon train, it occurs to me: this mare is as domesticated as a housecat. Did she wander away from her owners? Maybe her owner had a tragic accident and this horse was forced to make its way in the wilderness on its own. By the time I get back to camp, I've convinced myself that the gentle horse's owner was killed by the outlaws everybody fears. I'd better not mention that to anyone else.

It's been a couple of days since I saw Rose and Snarling Wolf. Usually, the shaman leaves Rose with us when he rides off on an adventure. Maybe they decided to follow the river while we cut out a bend in favor of a short cut. Will I ever stop worrying about that child? Just because she has a husband, should I stop being afraid for her? For a long time, I've worried about Rose's sanity, and the shaman she married doesn't seem to be any more sensible than she is. Maybe they're content to ride Snarling Wolf's horse doubled up, together. Rose never showed much of an interest in horseback riding, but if she's going to live among Indians, perhaps she should have a horse of her own. I wonder whether an Indian's mother-in-law is allowed to give her daughter a horse. Maybe the wagon master or his crew can answer that question for me.

Breathlessly, Andrew gushes, "You caught another wild horse, Mama?

Stillman's eyebrows form triangles on his forehead. "How do you do it?"

Christopher strokes the roan's neck with his good hand and she nuzzles his cheek. If Rose doesn't want the horse, maybe Christopher could have her. I'm surprised he hasn't begged for a pony or a horse of his own, come to think of it. My son scratches between her ears and then inspects the horse, making his way slowly around, and I realize that the sound he makes around the horse is similar to the voice I use to communicate with Blizzard. When he's done, he says. "She's lost. Her owner misses her. This horse has known hard times."

I stare into the innocent face of my son. Suddenly, he sounds as daft as Rose. I stutter to begin, repeating the windy sound of, "What?" several times before blurting, "What are you talking about, Christopher? How do you know? What makes you say that?"

He shrugs like it is yet another mystery that he doesn't care about, one way or another. "Dunno." A strange expression flashes across his face and he says, "Reverend Meadows claims that God talks to him. I'm not saying animals talk to me and yet, sometimes I feel like I can hear their thoughts. Isn't that the stupidest thing you ever heard of?" Christopher shrugs and laughs.

Behind me, Andrew says, "I can picture that horse. A skinny man rides her. His clothes are way too big for him. Just the thought of it gives me a headache." He rubs his temples and has a pained expression on his face.

Stillman says, "I have watch tonight. I'll take her to the picket line."

As I tie Blizzard to the back corner of our wagon and prepare for bed, I wish the boys goodnight and pray they're too tired to argue in the tent before falling asleep. What is wrong with me? I must be an awful parent. Rose claims to communicate with dead people. Andrew mysteriously knows what will happen before it does. I was beginning to think that Christopher was the only sane one and now he suggests that animals talk to him. Dahlia Jane can't remember having a stable home, but so far, she seems like an ordinary child. Do all parents think their offspring are strange? What if they were born ordinary, but it's my fault they turn crazy? And then there's Stillman. Good Heavens. We're all a bunch of freaks. What will become of us?

Friday, August 23

In the morning, it takes us an hour and a half to reunite with the Snake River. Rose and Snarling Wolf are camped there, waiting for our arrival. Snarling Wolf leaves Rose with us and rides off. When I ask her where he went, Rose shrugs. Either she doesn't know, or she chooses not to tell me.

After a couple more hours, trailing slightly south of the Snake, word passes along the line that we've reached the famous Three Island Crossing. How do the scouts decide to cross in one place versus another? We're told that this is a dangerous crossing, so why don't we cross somewhere else? They try to explain water currents and the slope of riverbanks. Why not cross from one riverbank to the other rather than from a riverbank to one island, then a second, and finally a third before crossing a wide stretch of water, finally to the opposite riverbank? Sometimes, there's no explaining what goes through a man's mind. It's as if they ponder for ages, finally discovering the worst possible solution to any given problem, and then go with that.

We're the seventh wagon in line today and I'm glad we're not the first to make the trip across the river. That honor goes to the single man, Schuyler Steele. Such a thought may not be fair, but I wish that each river would be traversed first by a single man. Families have much more to lose if a wagon fails to cross the river.

The journey across the river is time consuming. The first three wagons take an hour to make their way slowly from island to island before reaching the opposite shore. Beginning with the fourth wagon, our guides begin to move the wagons more quickly, such that we're preparing to make our way to the first island before the fourth wagon makes it to the northernmost bank.

Andrew doubles over like he's been punched in the gut. "I don't like it, Mama." He moans, "A picture of our wagon being swept away and smashed to bits flipped through my mind."

I gasp. "When?"

With a grimace, he answers, "Just now."

Urgently, I ask, "No, I mean when was it swept away? Which island?"

"That's just it. I didn't see any islands."

I look back and forth, unsure what to do. "What would you have me do, Andrew?"

He looks sick. "I don't know, Mama. Don't yell at me. I can't help it."

I whisper impatiently, "I'm sorry, dear. But I can't decide. Should I tell the scouts to be careful? They think it's funny when you guess the weather."

Andrew frowns. "Forget I mentioned it. Can we just be extra careful?"

The distance from the riverbank to the first island is one hundred yards, and the shallow water just covers the bottom quarter of the wagon wheels.

It's a relief to be on *terra firma* again. If only I could close my eyes and hold my breath as we cross to the second island. The water is deeper by several inches, but the distance to the second island is merely seventy-five yards.

We wait on the big island and watch as Stillman drives the wagon master's rig nine-hundred yards across the swift-moving river. Boss Wheel, Agapito, Arikta, and Dembi Koofai monitor the crossing from various vantage points, ready to come to the rescue as necessary. I'm relieved when Stillman completes his journey safely, but can't stop thinking about the worry in Andrew's voice when he told me about his vision. Boss Wheel's arm waves us forward and I speak to Andrew through clenched teeth. "Are we okay?"

He shrugs. "I guess."

I'm not reassured.

We wade into the fast current, up river from the wagon, in case disaster should strike. I pitch Dahlia Jane to my shoulders, so she can remain dry. Christopher cracks the whip and Scrapple pushes against the harness. The other oxen follow his lead. As we cross, I watch with worry as the water level climbs up the wagon wheels.

By the time we reach the middle of the river, the high water mark inches up the sides of the wagon bed. I'm glad we took the time to bolster the wagon, which adds to its height.

Beyond the midpoint, the water seems to move even more swiftly and the wagon wobbles. Christopher yells, cracks the whip, and the oxen pull harder. The wagon pitches from one direction to the other and looks to me like it might topple at any moment.

I want to shout a warning, but Andrew and Christopher are experts at this now. As the wagon climbs out of the river, I ask myself, *What was I thinking, letting a one armed, nine-year-old drive a team of oxen across the most accursed river at its most dangerous crossing, and after his spooky brother predicted a disaster, no less? I must be as crazy as the rest of my family.*

As we slowly make our way to the campsite for the evening, I sigh with relief. Water still drips from the moving wagon as Andrew reaches into a sagebrush and pulls a bird's nest from its branches. Dahlia Jane squirms as I lower her from my shoulders to my hip and she points at the nest made of grass, twigs, horsehair, and bark. She says, "Home."

Andrew says, "Yes. A green-tailed towhee lived in this nest. She had yellow wings, a white throat, and a red crown on the top of her head. What color tail do you think she had?"

Dahlia Jane blurts, "Green."

Andrew nods. "Good guess. You're pretty smart."

"Were there any eggs?"

He answers slowly, "Yes. There were four of them." A distant look appears on Andrew's face. "A man with bright blue eyes pinched the eggs and laughed as the yolks slipped through his fingers and globbed onto the ground."

I'm about to shush Andrew for fear of frightening Dahlia Jane, when reflected light off a shiny object beneath another shrub catches my eye. I swoop the object from the ground and the coarse shrub widens a tear in my sleeve, scratching my forearm. I say, "Look, children. It's a Jew's harp." I pass it to Andrew. "It's in pretty good condition, wouldn't you say?"

Andrew nods and passes it to Rose.

Rose lifts it to her lips, bites down on the tines, and plucks the trigger. I wish she had washed it before putting it in her mouth. At first, it makes an awkward sound. Then, she tips her head back slightly and the harp delivers a delightful twang. With a satisfied grunt, Rose passes it back to me and I slip it into my pocket.

After supper, we pass the instrument around and everyone takes a turn making sounds with it. Stillman is the last to try and quickly finds proficiency with the u-shaped instrument. There's no accounting for the emergence of talent, but Stillman is quickly able to deliver pleasing sounds from the mouth harp.

At the end of the evening, Rose climbs aboard the prairie schooner as if it is still a part of her ordinary routine. All night, she never looked around for Snarling Wolf. It is as if she knew that he wouldn't be along today. To me, it is a blissful return to the not too distant past. Whether it is a day, now and then, or more frequent than that, I'll take what I can get.

As we settle in to seek sleep, Rose speaks. "Have you ever heard of Sacagawea, Mama?"

I yawn and ask, "Do you mean the woman who helped guide Lewis and Clark on their expedition?"

"Yes, Mama. Do you remember when I told you about my spirit guide, Janey?"

"I do."

"Captain Clark called Sacagawea, Janey. Sacagawea is my guardian angel, Mama. Good night."

How preposterous. That's utterly absurd. The farther we get from home, the madder we seem to get.

SATURDAY, AUGUST 24

IN THE MORNING, ANDREW and I are alone for a few minutes as we get ready to depart toward the northwest.

I say, "So that's the end of the Snake then? Are we safe now?"

He shakes his head and rubs his nose. "No, Mama. They say we'll leave the Snake River for a while, and cross its path once more."

Trying to picture it in my mind hurts my head. I protest, "But I don't understand. If we're going that way, and it's going over there, and we followed it from that direction, how can we cross it again, ahead?"

He tosses a shoulder and says, "They say you never can tell which end of the Snake is which, Mama. I can draw you a map. Maybe I could put it in the newspaper."

I nod. "Sounds like a good idea to me, Andrew. That would help a lot. I think everyone would appreciate that."

Rose steps from the wagon and approaches our tiny campfire. It's just big enough to make coffee and porridge. Andrew says, "I'll get the oxen."

I turn to Rose and say, "About yesterday, dear."

She snaps, "What about it?"

Gently, I say, "Do you remember what you told me last night?"

Rose groans. "Of course, Mama. Do you think I'm an idiot?"

"No, dear. What I'm wondering is, if Sacagawea has always been your guardian angel, why are you telling me now?"

"Oh, that. She wants to warn us about the danger ahead. She thinks I should have told you about her a long time ago, but I wanted to keep her to myself."

I stammer, searching for something appropriate to say. Rose's words often leave me speechless. "Can you tell me anything more about Sacagawea's warning?" For a non-believer in such doings, suddenly I'm eager for specificity when it comes to my children's supernatural suggestions.

Rose turns until she's almost facing me. It looks like she's thinking or trying to remember. "I don't know, Mama. She isn't always clear, but she makes the sign for *snake* and says the word over and over again. She's not talking about the Shoshone Indians, because that's not the word she uses for her people."

"Can you ask her what we should do, next time she talks to you?"

Rose shakes her head gently and then turns away. It's as if she thinks I've asked a stupid question. "That's not how it works, Mama."

Dahlia Jane calls from the back of the wagon. I suppose if the ghosts wish us to know more, they shall have to tell us. Rose doesn't seem to have more to say about the matter. I guess if one is to set out and conjure up an imaginary friend, why choose an ordinary one when the possibilities are endless. Sacagawea, indeed! Good Heavens!

In the middle of the afternoon when the wagons circle, hours before sunset, we're surprised by the choice of campground. The hideous trickle of a creek is described as Cold Spring Creek. By late summer, it is barely a dribble and nobody wants to spend one night here, let alone a long, dreary Sunday.

Galusha Gains, Samuel Grosvenor, and Horace Blocker descend upon Boss Wheel, but Galusha does most of the talking.

In a booming voice, the angry hunter challenges our chief guide. "Why did we stop at this God forsaken trickle after only thirteen miles of travel?"

The wagon boss says, "Because you can't make it twenty-six miles in one day to the next God forsaken trickle in your weary condition."

Samuel says, "But I don't want to spend two days here."

Boss Wheel grumbles and says, "Me neither. You'll have to take that objection to a higher authority."

In an abnormally high voice, Horace squeaks, "Can you promise we'll clear the Blue Mountains before it snows?"

"No. Nobody can tell about the weather. Snow can come early, or it can come late."

Galusha grunts. "We gotta stop wasting time. Winter's coming fast and we're moving slowly."

Boss Wheel adjusts his hat and says, "You pilgrims need to talk to your Captain. At this pace, I'd guess there's a good chance you'll make it in time and a good chance you will not."

After listening to Boss Wheel, and hearing the children's warnings, I'm unsure. I'm never one to agree with that bunch, but if I were to cast a vote at this moment, I'd have to throw in with them.

When the men gather in a tight ring around The Hub, our women surround them. Captain Meadows is not moved by arguments against traveling on Sunday. He leans forward and pontificates, "If there's a chance that it could snow before we reach the mountains, then we must strengthen our appeal to the Lord's good graces rather than offend Him. Who among us can stop the snow from falling, or cause the snow to fall if he wishes? Only the Lord has such powers. If these mountains are as fearsome as you suggest, then we need these days of rest and prayer, now more than ever. As long as I'm the Captain in charge of this venture, we shall observe the Sabbath."

Galusha shouts into the crowd. "Let's choose a new Captain. I'll take the job if you want me to." The man looks at me. "If I won't do, you can elect Samuel, here."

I agree with the challengers about traveling on Sundays. As a woman, I'm not entitled to vote, but if it were up to me, I would not vote to replace Captain Meadows with the weasel or the skunk. I'd rather take my chances on the Heavens than be led by Galusha Gains or Samuel Grosvenor, even if the skunk were to spend a couple of hours with a bar of soap in the river. Stillman looks at me before casting his vote, shrugs, and supports Captain Meadows.

When I return to the wagon, Rose is gone. I look at Andrew and he points up the trickling creek. Rose and Snarling Wolf are holding hands, and in a blink, they disappear behind a hillside.

Sunday, August 25

Sunday afternoon, when the baking and wash are done, I saddle Blizzard and ride off alone to the northeast, following the creek in the direction of the mountains. When I return dragging a scrawny shrub, I'm surprised to see pandemonium in camp. With a click of my tongue and a squeeze of my legs, I nudge Blizzard forward at a faster pace. Children run all about, as if they're playing a game. Hastily, I tie Blizzard to the outer corner of our wagon and race around to the other side.

For weeks, Stillman has been crafting a new cage from whittled sticks, twigs, and woven fibers. The oddly shaped result is nearing completion. With all the discarded belongings we've seen along the way, it should have been possible to find a proper, abandoned cage and we've been on the lookout for a while, to no avail. As Gloria's chicks have matured, the box that once looked spacious barely provides sufficient space for the creatures to move. We've had several offers from neighbors to trade for chickens, but have declined them all.

My voice squeaks when I ask, "What happened, Stillman?"

He puts a hand on his cheek and answers, "It's hard to say. I brought the crate down to clean it. Then, I went to get a shovel. When I returned, the cage door was open and the squawking chickens were making off in every direction." With a wild gesture, Stillman's hands wave all about as if directing the children's chase. "And then, this happened."

Herding chickens isn't hard. They generally move in whatever direction they're nudged in. The tricky part is capturing them. Their flight instinct propels them forward, just beyond arm's reach. Rounding them up is easiest when there's a corner to trap them into. Then, they can be grabbed with a swift, deliberate pair of hands. On the range and among the wagons, there are no likely places to ambush escaped pullets.

The wild throng of barbaric children relish the challenge and the adults seem content to allow the disruptive contest between predators and prey. In most wagon camps, they sit, relaxing, and cheer the children on without providing assistance.

Some of the children look exhausted. I ask, "How long has this been going on, Stillman?"

His lips shift from one side to the other and it looks like he's trying to remember, or calculate. "Not long. Maybe ten minutes before you rode up."

Our friend from home, the painter Bacon Bump, trots forward from his wagon waving a net on a stick. The pliable trap doesn't look to be large enough to contain a chicken, but who knows? He hands it to Robbie Prindle, then leans against The Hub and watches the scrambling children chase the terrified poultry as if memorizing the scene. Perhaps he'll make a painting of the incident later.

Bacon's net provides just enough extra reach to even the odds. Maybe the children have worn the flock down. One by one, the birds are captured until we have a cage full of chickens again, only nobody can find the hen that mothered the flock and warmed them since they hatched, back in April. There's no place to hide on the open range and the exhausted children have given up their search. Dahlia Jane is distraught. "Where's Gloria? We have to find her. We can't give up." She blinks fast, her lip curls, and tears can't be far off.

I suggest, "Let's take a break, dear. Maybe if we settle down for a few minutes, she'll get bored of hiding and reveal herself."

After a couple of impatient hours, the inconsolable child fails to convince other children to renew the search. Dahlia Jane turns to me and says, "What if she ran away? We'll never see her again. Do you think Gloria wandered out there?" Dahlia Jane points off toward the mountains.

Hoping to distract her, I offer, "Let's saddle up and take a ride. Maybe we'll find her." Is it possible that the missing chicken stepped off undetected while the children pursued the rest of the flock? I pat her head and say, "Stay with Stillman. I'll get the new horse."

We follow the creek to the northeast. I don't really expect to find Gloria, but making the trip placates Dahlia Jane, at least temporarily. We ride into Rose's camp and I pass Dahlia Jane to Snarling Wolf before sliding off. Breathlessly, the child tells her sister about our search. "We can't find Gloria anywhere. Have you seen her? Did she come this way?"

Rose shakes her head and Snarling Wolf tells Dahlia Jane that he hasn't seen the chicken either. The child says, "Gloria misses her home. She just wants to go back. Do you think she's trying to get back home?"

I say, "I don't think chickens are that smart, dear."

Dahlia Jane is not pleased with my assessment. She pouts and says, "How can we make cake without Gloria?"

The child's love of cake is known to all. "Gloria's chicks will start laying soon. It won't be long until we have more eggs than we know what to do with."

She frowns, unconvinced. "Let's keep looking."

Rose says, "Hope you find her before the wagons set out in the morning."

A look of horror crosses Dahlia Jane's face. "We can't leave Gloria here, Mama. If we don't find her, I'm not going."

Children can be stubborn. I'm not looking forward to tomorrow's departure.

On the way back to the wagon train, we cross the path of a gray wolf. Lone wolves normally keep their distance, particularly in the daytime. I scream when I see the creature and desperately cover Dahlia Jane's eyes with my hand. The poor squawking bundle of feathers is unable to escape the wolf's jaws.

Dahlia Jane screeches. "Shoot it, Mama. Shoot it hard."

I kick the gentle mare and we race back to the wagon train. My grip on Dahlia Jane is so tight, she screams. "You're hurting me, Mama."

As we dismount, I apologize. "I'm sorry, dear. I didn't mean to squash you and I'm sorry we couldn't save Gloria."

Monday, August 26

LAST NIGHT, IT TOOK forever to get Dahlia Jane to fall asleep. I was supposed to stand watch, but Dahlia Jane refused to let me go. I had to ask Stillman to take my place. The bereft child cried for almost two hours before she finally drifted off. Then, I couldn't fall asleep. Thoughts of the gruesome, chicken killing creature kept returning to my mind whenever my eyes closed.

Maybe I got a few minutes of sleep before Dahlia Jane woke up screaming. She must have awakened half the camp with her screaming fits of night terrors. Finally, through her sobs, she conveyed her nightmare which sounded identical to my recurring wolf dream. "There there, child." I held her close to my bosom, stroked her hair, and whispered soothing notions to her. She managed to drift off for a couple of minutes at a time, always waking up a few minutes later with the same vivid dream.

Twice during the night, there was a scratch of fingernails against the canvas wagon bonnet. "Is our flower alright, *estimada*?"

I managed to garble the words, "It is just a nightmare. Nothing more." I have always hated that phrase, *just a nightmare*. Anyone who suffers from the same terrifying dream, over and over again, knows the horror of such an experience.

Morning has finally come, and I'm glad. Though I didn't get any sleep, my back and arms are sore from holding Dahlia Jane all night. The only way I could keep her quiet was to cradle her. She remains asleep when I set her on a stack of folded quilts, and the sound of Agapito's blasted trumpet doesn't wake her either.

When my feet hit the ground, I stretch and yawn so hard, my eyes water. I don't care if I use the last of the firewood or have to burn Stillman's hand-made birdcage. I must have coffee. After rubbing my eyes, I commence to building a fire and set the pot at the edge of its flames.

While Andrew fetches the oxen, I stride to The Hub and retrieve the post. I encounter Cian, who says, "Did you find that missing chicken?" He licks his lips and adds, "I wouldn't mind some fried chicken about now. Sure enough."

I tell him about seeing the wolf carry Gloria away, and shudder at the thought of the wild beast ripping the poor chicken apart and feasting on its bones.

Cian says, "Pity, that. A fine meal, gone to waste." He pulls half a roll from his pocket, nibbles a tiny bite from its edge, and returns the remainder to his pocket.

My mouth waters at the thought. It has been a long time since we have enjoyed a meal of fried chicken. Somehow, the wolf who steals a chicken is a wicked beast, whereas a thigh dipped in buttermilk and coated with flour, sizzling in oil, is domestic bliss. My stomach growls and I frown at the thought of having mush for breakfast again today.

We have a short march of thirteen miles from Cold Springs Creek to Hot Springs Creek, yet I can't wait to get there. The whole day is one continuous yawn fest. I'm too tired to fix a meal when we stop for our mid-day break. I spread a dusty blanket on the dirt and sit on it. I tell myself I just need a minute and then I'll get the children something to eat from the wagon. Somehow, I manage to fall asleep and Christopher shakes my shoulder. "Wake up, Mama. It's time to go."

With a startled grunt, I labor to climb to my feet. "Good Heavens, child. I'm sorry."

Despite the nap, I'm not refreshed. I look about, feeling disoriented. I barely make it to my feet before Christopher whips the blanket away with his good arm and crumples it up in an unfolded heap, tossing it into the back of the wagon. Stumbling along behind the departing rig, all I can think about is folding that darn blanket. I'm not that good a housekeeper, that such a thing should stick in my head. The truth is, I'm more like Christopher in that regard than I'd like to admit. How could he fold the blanket with one arm in a sling? Why can't I stop thinking about that stupid quilt? There's no telling why such notions get trapped in the head, especially when sleep is scarce.

Finally, I step up my pace, retrieve the blanket, and fold it while walking. Then, I must hurry again to place the folded bedding back in the wagon. Having accomplished the task, I acknowledge to myself that its completion doesn't make me feel any different, but at least the nagging thought of dishevelment is gone. Some days are like this. We don't seem to accomplish much worth remembering or recounting. I wonder what Andrew will write about in today's issue of *The Rolling Home Times*.

My fellow travelers grumble at the short trek. I suppose we must stop here, because this is where the water is. Somewhere to the northeast there is supposed to be a blissful spring where we can warm our weary bodies and soak in invigorating mineral baths. I'm normally the first to want to check out each novel landmark and the opportunity to bathe is also a pleasant prospect, but today, I just don't care. I barely have the energy to make it through the most basic of chores and struggle to stay awake until dusk. When it is finally time to crawl aboard and retreat for the evening, I'm relieved.

Usually, when I tell Dahlia Jane a story, she hangs on every word. Tonight, I babble incoherently while my fingers rub my eyes. The child flips and flops a few times and, while sitting on a small barrel, I look at my quilt, yearning to stretch out. Couldn't I finish the story from a supine position? As I make myself comfortable, I realize that I'm not telling a story at all. I'm merely saying my thoughts out loud. It doesn't matter. Dahlia Jane is fast asleep.

Closing my eyes is Heavenly bliss. I've never felt so relaxed. When Dahlia Jane wakes, screaming again, I sit up fast, disoriented. Where am I? Are we under attack? I have the feeling of waking up lost. Then, I realize my baby has the night terrors again. With a groan, I realize that it's going to be another long night.

Tuesday, August 27

Our next stop is at Rattlesnake Creek. It's hard to look forward to arriving at a place with such a name, but after another sleepless night, who cares where we park our rig? I imagine I could fall asleep anywhere and sleep through my worst nightmares.

Doctor Appleyard assures me that Dahlia Jane will get over her night terrors, given time, and I hope he's right. She spends all day talking about chickens and playing with the bird's nest that Andrew found at Three Island Crossing. She even has a clutch of egg shaped rocks at the bottom of the nest and speaks of the tumble of twigs as home.

Nothing of substance crosses my mind as I place one foot in front of the other and watch the wagon wheels turn beside me. When the wagons circle, late in the afternoon, I climb onto the wagon and close my eyes. The children must fend for themselves. Hopefully, somebody is watching Dahlia Jane. Hours before dark, I'm fast asleep.

At supper, The Viper says, "It ain't enough. We gotta have more." He un-leashes a string of profanities, and then continues. "Today, the longest wagon train we ever saw passed through here and all we managed to get our hands on was horses."

Sloan says, "The more wagons there are, the more guns we gotta go up against."

The Radish clarifies, "Three horses."

The Viper hates to agree with Sloan, but his brother is right. It seems like the caravans have grown longer and longer since they started in the business of hunting fortunes along The Oregon Trail. After almost a decade, news of the dangers has spread and greenhorns gather together in ever greater numbers, to run the gauntlet more safely.

The blue eyed mastermind rubs the stubble on his chin and contemplates. How many wagons were in today's procession?

Usually, The Viper counts the wagons with precision, but today he lost count. Was it a hundred? Two hundred? Could there have been even more than that? He frowns at the recollection that he couldn't see point and drag at the s ame time.

The expression on his face becomes pained. Every wagon is valuable. Some-times, they discover gold, bank notes, coins, or jewelry. Other times, they harvest provisions. Even the poorest emigrants travel with something of value. The Viper thinks it is a waste to let such valuable riches just roll on by.

Today, the targeted wagons traveled evenly spaced. Usually, there are breaks. Most times, as the wagons stretch out, slower wagons fall behind. That's when opportunity knocks. But today, the wagons traveled slow and steady. One wagon followed the next as if they were chained together. The only opportunity that The Viper saw was to pick off some stock. The Viper looks at his brothers with a critical eye. Sloan isn't good for much, but The Radish is another story.

The Viper grumbles. "Just three miserable plugs. Such a pity."

Stealing horses is The Radish's specialty. The Viper usually praises his youngest brother's stealth. But today, The Viper isn't pleased with their take.

The Radish issues a rare protest. "Ain't horses worth something? A man can grind for half a year to afford just one. Today, we got three."

With a sour expression on his face, The Viper repeats. "It ain't enough. Not for boys with expensive tastes." He spits out the last two words with venomous disdain.

Sloan slumps and says, "You can't be talking about me. Expensive tastes? Pshaw!"

The Viper sneers. "I don't think you understand how much it costs to sit around and do nothing. Even cheap whiskey don't come for free. In civilization, it costs money to have a roof over your head and a bunk beneath your back. And, you want to eat, don't you?"

Sloan chuckles. "You'd better believe it. I've had enough beans to last a lifetime." Sloan lets off a noxious cloud of gas, punctuating his point. "When we're rich, I'm eating nothing but steak. No more rotten, stinking beans for me ."

The Radish's nose crinkles as if offended by the smell. "Can't we just take the stock? Why you always gotta kill people?"

The Viper bends at the waist, leans forward, and raises his voice. He doesn't usually yell at his brothers, but now his voice thunders in their ears. "We're far from the law out here and we ain't never safe. Out here, there's a hero with a gun hiding around every bend of the river, each with his own sense of justice." The Viper smacks one hand in his other, repeatedly chopping into his palm. "People talk. Word spreads. If somebody sees us and describes what we look like, people gonna come looking. Maybe somebody's gonna draw pictures of us. It's better if nobody knows where we are, how many of us there is, or what we look like." The Viper stomps a heavy boot heel on the ground. "We g ot work to do, boys. We'd better get on with it."

The grumbling brothers begin to move.

The Viper barks. "I've had enough of talking. Git a move on. Now."

The Radish trips Sloan as he scrambles from the porch. Sloan tumbles to the ground and promptly musters the energy to spring to his feet. Sloan jumps at The Radish and The Viper watches his brothers wrestle in the dust. There ain't a reason for it, except that it's been too long since the brothers had a q uality tussle.

The Viper's hands grip his belly and his cheeks tighten as the pain in his churning gut registers in his head. Dunderheads. What's the point? Time is *wasting away. Why can't they understand? The seasons are going to change again soon. The Viper knows he could easily stop the boys from fighting. Sometimes, young men need to waste time and energy on such foolishness. All he would need to do is raise his voice and they'd obediently jump to their feet, as they always do. Instead, The Viper lowers his backside to the edge of the p rch and closes his eyes.* Why do I bother? They're never grateful. They don't appreciate all I do for them. But they're too dumb to survive on their own. I should just let them go. *The pain in The Viper's gut doubles at the thought, but he continues thinking it anyway.* I've painted a mighty pretty picture for them, but I don't want to live that life. I've got everything I want right here. Why should we have to leave? Why can't this place be enough for them? I can't stand the idiots, so why can't I live without them?

When The Viper opens his eyes, his brothers are standing in front of him, dusty and disheveled, hats in hands, but no worse for the brawling.

"You get that out of your system now?"

The boys nod.

"Now, let's get outta here."

Wednesday, August 28

It was a good thing I slept before dark last night, because Dahlia Jane woke up three times last night, screaming like a banshee. It's the third night in a row. Finally, I ask her about her nightmares. "Tell me what you see. Maybe it will help, dear. Is it wolves?"

The child sniffles and talks slowly while looking at her doll. "Sometimes. There are four of them. But there is also a golden snake." Dahlia Jane cries, clutches the ragdoll to her chest, and can't continue.

Reaching for her hand, I say, "There there, child. Try not to worry."

When she asks me to carry her, I oblige. Larkin isn't here to bellyache about coddling the children, but I have to admit, Dahlia Jane feels heavier than she used to. After a while, I set her in the back of the wagon and let her play.

I'm surprised when Horace Blocker wanders up to me. I can't remember him leaving his wagon while traveling. I ask, "Is Lana driving the oxen today, Horace?"

"No. Adam is." Horace and Lana's son is eight, just a year younger than Christopher, but Adam is small for his age. "Of course, Lana is there too. I had to get away."

All of a sudden, the man begins a rant. Why did he choose to share his grumblings with me? Perhaps everyone else knows better than to greet Horace Blocker and start asking questions.

He shouts at me like I'm forcing him to go on. "I can't take it anymore. Hour after hour, we march like soldiers. These stupid beasts move so slowly. We're on a snail's pace to nowhere. I'm bored out of my mind. Every day something terrible happens. We're all going to die. I just know it."

Glancing about, I beg, "Please Horace, you'll scare the children."

Snidely, he says, "I don't give a hang what the children think. One day is too hot and the next day we freeze." Horace cracks his knuckles so violently I'm afraid he'll break off his fingers.

His hands join behind his back and he says, "I have half a mind to dig myself a grave, climb in, and pull the dirt in over me. I don't think I can go any farther. I hope the Indians attack us and put me out of my misery. If the outlaws come for us, I hope they shoot me first. We're all going to suffer miserable deaths anyway. What difference does it make, how we go? Why put it off?"

Resisting the impulse to slap some sense into the man, I raise my voice. "Snap out of it, Horace. Lana and Adam depend on you. Yes, it is hard, but we must persevere." I try to think how I can turn the naysayer's thoughts in a positive direction. It would help if I knew him better. "If you could have anything in the world, Horace, what would it be?"

"Oh, if I had magic powers, just think of what I could do." He waves his finger like a magic wand. "If only there were such a thing as conjuring. Poof, there's a peach tree. Bam, an apple tree. Wah! A guest house. We should never have left Georgia."

Encouraged, I hope to keep Horace on the sunny side. "Did you have a peach tree in Georgia? I have never seen one. The only peaches I've ever seen came in a can, packed in syrup."

The man looks at me and his face sags. "God, I miss them. If only I could conjure myself back to Georgia." He shakes a finger in front of his face and says, "Poof." Then he looks sadly back at me. "No, I might as well face it. It's hopeless. We're all going to die."

I clear my throat and say, "I wish you'd stop saying that. It's very upsetting." How can I get the gloomy grump to think differently? "Tell me something else, Horace. What does Lana want? More than anything, what does she wish for?"

His shoulders droop as he answers. "A little girl. It's all she's *ever* wanted: a little girl with pigtails."

"What about your boy? What does he want?" I try to think of Adam and can't remember much about him despite the months we've traveled the same trail. He doesn't say much and looks about as miserable as his father.

Horace scratches behind his ear and speaks while exhaling. "Fishing." He takes a deep breath and continues. "All he ever wants to do is go fishing. We pass all these rivers and he always begs to dangle a hook in the water. We send him to fetch water and he never comes back. He's always fishing, but there's never anything on his line. I keep telling him he has to use bait if he want to hook anything. Kid takes after his mother, he ain't too smart." Horace pauses for a moment, wags his finger, and says, "Poof, a picnic. How about that, lady? Can your daughter do that?"

"What do you mean?"

"Your daughter, the witch. Can she conjure up a feast? Wouldn't that be something? I wish I could."

"My daughter is not a witch. Stop saying that. Where did you get such an idea?"

"From that Irish lass, Oona Reid. She said your daughter conjured up a wild Indian who brings her fresh meat every night, just like magic. Tomorrow, you will all have to go on without the Blockers. Wherever our wheels stop tonight, that's home. I can't go on. Not one more mile. Ya hear me? Not one more mile. It's time to hang up my fiddle."

I look around. Nobody can live here, especially not alone. And certainly not Horace Blocker. Boss Wheel's words come to mind. This is the part of the journey where all of the greenhorns turn loco.

Why should I try to reform this man? He's beyond help anyway. The miserable cur never had one nice thing to say to me and has the nerve to tell me that he thinks my daughter is a witch. It would be like sprinkling sugar on a turd. There's no way to sweeten up a man like Horace Blocker.

Poor Lana and Adam.

THURSDAY, AUGUST 29

THE SCREECHING VOICE OF a wailing woman catches my ear and I race toward the sound. Ten yards from The Hub, Horace stands holding a Bowie knife. Cian Reid stands a short distance away. Horace shouts, "I'm going to slice off your ear and make you eat it. How do you like that, foreigner?" The way he says *foreigner* conveys disgust.

Oona wails again. Her fists tug at her strawberry blond hair. She howls, "Stop that lunatic before he kills somebody."

Horace stomps his feet.

Cian steps back, trying to distance himself from the man who insults him. He clumsily trips. It's as if a root were conjured from the soil, hooking his ankle. The Irishman lands in the dirt on his backside.

Boss Wheel and his crew appear on the scene. The trail boss barks, "What is the meaning of this?"

Horace screeches. "I caught that burglar robbing our wagon and stealing our food."

Cian crawls backward through the dust. "Explain, I can. I'm no burglar. It's all a mistake, I promise you. So sorry. I was confused. In a daze, I was. After a while, the back of one wagon looks the same as the next, you see. Forgive me." He holds up his arms as if Horace were brandishing a revolver instead of a knife.

Boss Wheel steps forward.

Horace waves the twelve inch blade in the wagon master's direction. "Stand back, Frenchie, or I'll plant this blade in your heart. That, or you can shoot me. I don't care which. If I had the guts, I'd stab myself, but I'll not have this shanty-dwelling donkey in my wagon. Keep that pig away from my family, or I'll gut him, if it's the last thing I do."

Cian gulps and he shakes his hands in the air as if trying to prove that he didn't steal anything. "No, it was an accident. I swear. It could happen to anybody. Forgive me, you must."

I'm surprised that Horace has the energy, or gumption, to wag a blade at people. From talking with the man yesterday, I believe he wants nothing more than to have the wagon master, or a crew member, shoot him and put him out of his misery. As for Cian, I'm sorry that he knew such hunger in his youth. He isn't above begging, but I don't believe he is a thief, and he sure doesn't deserve to get his ear sliced off.

Finally, fast talking Agapito convinces Horace to set his knife down and accept the Irishman's apology. The crowd of onlookers disperses and I think about Horace's threat to discontinue his journey to Oregon. He didn't follow through this morning when we departed from Rattlesnake Creek. Did the man forget? Was he just blustering? Does he still intend to drop anchor somewhere in the wilderness?

Andrew and Christopher bicker when we get back to camp.

Andrew shakes a jaw at his brother and says, "You didn't do your share today, Christopher. You can do extra tomorrow."

Christopher pulls his hat from his head and hurls it at the ground. It's clear to see the anger on his twisted up face. "No way, Andrew. We're last in line tomorrow. We'll be eating dust all day. I'm not doing it. This morning, you told me to get lost, so I did. I'm through with having you boss me around all the time."

"I didn't mean for you to disappear all day." Andrew groans. "I just wanted you to quit pestering me."

Christopher kicks his hat. "I don't pester you, Andrew. I don't talk to you at all, if I can help it. You can spend all day writing things down if you want to. I don't care if you make a newspaper or not. I ain't gonna step and fetch for you so you can scribble junk on paper. I want to live life, not read about it. I want to do things, not write down all of the stuff other people do. I want to hunt, fish, shoot, dig, and ride, just like Alvah does."

Andrew rolls his eyes. "There you go. Alvah, Alvah, Alvah. That's all you ever talk about and I'm sick of hearing it. That's what I mean about pestering. How about if you're going to run your mouth, maybe you could find something new or interesting to say for a change."

Christopher raises his good arm in the air and jabs at nothing with his open hand. "Interesting? You have no idea what's *interesting*. How about instead of going on for pages about Bacon Bump's butterfly collection, you write exciting things down? You didn't even mention the day the chickens escaped and poor Gloria got eaten by a wolf. All's I saw was a boring interview about old lady Knox's favorite recipes."

"That's disrespectful, Christopher." Andrew looks around to see who is listening. With his hands on his waist, Andrew says, "Garland's great aunt Hannah's jams and jellies took first place at the county fair."

Christopher tosses his head in a circular motion. "Ho, hum."

"Everybody has their own passions, Christopher. I want to interview everybody on the wagon train. I can't just publish Alvah, Alvah, Alvah interviews every day. Do you think Hannah Knox wants to read about Alvah Nye's shotgun?"

"Who cares? Nobody reads that newspaper anymore anyway."

I've had enough. It's time to intervene. "Christopher, that's not very nice."

Andrew turns his back on his younger brother. "No, Mama. He's right. It's true. People only care about made up stories. They don't care about what *really* happens. I ought to just quit wasting my time. Nobody cares anyway."

The wagon boss steps into our camp. That never happens. I'm flabbergasted when he says, "I used to fight with my brother. I ain't seen him in years. Can't remember what we used to fight about, but I miss him. Think of that. And, another thing... that blame newspaper is a thorn in my side sometimes, but I guarantee you, someday it will provide a priceless record. Treasure it. As for Alvah Nye, a boy couldn't have a better hero."

The crusty, former mountain man looks at me and mockingly says, "Good Heavens." He wriggles his torso as if to pretend he has the figure of a woman. Then he says, "Wherever did I learn to be such a busybody?"

Friday, August 30

In the morning, Andrew is the first one awake and we have a few minutes together before anyone else joins us. He says, "I try to be nice to everybody, Mama. Even Christopher. He made me so angry yesterday. Do you think I'm mean to him?"

In a soft voice that I hope he'll find reassuring, I say, "Sometimes, it is hard to be the younger brother. Nobody likes to be told what to do, and you and Christopher are very different people."

Andrew rolls his tongue over his teeth, contemplatively. The tone of his voice sounds like somebody recalling days long gone by. "He never used to mind doing what I told him to do. What happened? Something changed."

"Maybe it did. This journey has made him realize what he likes. Whether he knows it or not, I think he learned how to pursue his passions from you, Andrew. When you're interested in something, you give it everything you've got. Now, I've noticed, Christopher does that too. He used to follow you like a shadow, but he's outgrowing that."

"What did you think of what Boss Wheel said, Mama?"

"I agree with everything he said. Though I never expected a man such as him to say anything like that. Did you?"

"No. It was a little bit surprising. I was going to quit the newspaper business until he came over. Now, I don't know what to do."

"Andrew, I should have stopped Christopher. He should not have said those things about the paper."

"He was right, Mama. I hated to hear it, but I knew it was true as soon as he said it. It felt like a slap in the face. I can't remember anything hurting so much. I wanted to cry, but I didn't. I'm too old for that."

"I disagree. You're never too old to cry. Sometimes things seem clearer after you let your emotions loose, but what do I know? I don't let myself cry often enough. As for the newspaper, Andrew, I agree with Boss Wheel. I'd hate to see you stop now. You're creating something so valuable, we may never know just how important your work is. Please, don't stop."

"But who cares about Hannah Knox's preserves?" He tips his head forward and his lower lip juts forward. "My own mother doesn't even read *The Rolling Home Times*."

"Oh, she doesn't, does she? Then she can't be very smart. But, I will have you know, I did read it yesterday, Andrew, and I agree with you. I may not enjoy Hannah Knox any more than Christopher does, but I think your interview did its job. You should chronicle the occupants of all thirty-one wagons. Let the readers decide which interviews they want to read. Christopher looks up to Alvah, and that's wonderful, but maybe someone else will want to emulate Hannah Knox. There's just no telling."

"What about Horace Blocker, Mama? I'm afraid to print the story about how he threatened Cian Reid with a knife, but it is news." Andrew flinches and draws a hand to his abdomen. "Should a newspaperman publish a story even if he is afraid of getting stabbed?"

"Horace Blocker is not going to stab you, dear. I think you should interview everyone involved and make sure you give the man a chance to tell his side of the story. Isn't that how journalism works?"

"I suppose. I never met a newspaperman, so I guess I'm just making up how to do it. Do you think I could interview him? I've already interviewed almost everybody else."

I'm not sure Horace Blocker will consent to an interview, but I tell Andrew that he should ask the man. Then, I ask, "What about Boss Wheel? Did you interview him? I can't remember. Maybe I missed an issue." The truth is, I've missed far too many issues of the newspaper. I should do better.

Andrew says, "I tried. He told me he was too busy for such nonsense."

"You should try again now. After what he said yesterday, how could he refuse you? I don't know what's come over him. It's as if the man went to bed one night and woke up the next day, transformed. It's quite remarkable, really. I'll bet Boss Wheel could tell you things about the wilderness you never imagined. He might provide you with days worth of material."

Christopher steps from the tent and Stillman rolls from his blankets beneath the wagon. Dahlia Jane is still asleep. Last night, she only awakened once. Hopefully, the frightful memory of Gloria's tragic demise has begun to fade from my daughter's mind.

As the wagon train departs from Ditto Creek and travels toward Slater Creek, each step feels the same as the one before and each day is hard to tell from those gone by. Yet, every day is unique. I think of Horace Blocker, tempting fate by wishing for his own demise. Every day is worth living. Someday, I look forward to sitting down and reading Andrew's newspapers, one after the other. Imagine, sitting in a comfortable chair or reclining on a plush mattress, reading about a grueling journey, many years after voyaging. It's hard to fathom ever knowing the comforts of civilization, this far removed from any city, town, or village.

Whenever we pass clumps of sagebrush, we hack away at any brittle branches we can find, desperate for something to burn in the evening. One creek looks much the same as another. We should be grateful for any tributary that features drinkable water, but it would be nice to find a body of water deep enough to provide an opportunity to bathe.

When I carry a pail to Slater Creek for a bucket of water, I'm surprised to see Boss Wheel on his knees, kneading his capote in the river. There's a coarse burlap sack beside the man. I wonder whether it holds other garments he plans to wash, or could it contain the contents of the deep pockets of his long cloak? It never occurred to me that the man would do his own washing.

SATURDAY, AUGUST 31

THERE'S WIDESPREAD GRUMBLING WHEN we circle at another miserable trickle. Perhaps it's a respectable waterway in the springtime, but there's not much to mention about it at the end of August. It's not the sort of place where weary travelers want to spend one night, let alone two, but the next source of water is thirty miles up the path. What choice do we have?

Stillman, Christopher, and I set up camp and tend the chores while Andrew sits on a box and rubs his temples. "It's not just my head, Mama. My stomach aches, and I feel like I have saddle sores."

Unsympathetically, Christopher says, "Buck up. You only spent a couple of hours in the saddle and that gentle roan never more than walked."

Andrew groans and pulls his palm across his face. "I can't help it."

When the chores are finished, Christopher announces that he intends to visit Alvah, Honey, and the puppies. Dahlia Jane begs to accompany him and the boy begrudgingly takes his baby sister along. Stillman grabs a sack and wanders off in search of burnable scraps. Andrew and I are left alone.

The color of his skin doesn't look right. I say, "Should I get the doctor, dear?"

He pulls his hat over his forehead as if trying to disappear. "No, Mama," he groans.

Stepping toward the water barrel with a tumbler, I ask, "Are you thirsty?"

"I suppose."

As I lower the dipper into the barrel, I inquire, "Do you think you have the same thing I had a week ago?"

Andrew leans forward at the waist. Maybe a different position will make him feel better. He answers, "I don't think so. Wasn't that sunstroke? It's not so hot anymore."

The heat spell has broken but the temperature cooks us in the afternoon. It doesn't seem likely that Andrew got through the heat spell without coming down with sunstroke, only to have it now, but there's no telling what can happen where the human body is concerned. I beg Andrew to drink as often as he can, just to be sure. Then, I ask him to tell me about his afternoon with Boss Wheel. "What if you were writing a newspaper article for a fancy newspaper back east? How would you describe the man?"

"I don't know, Mama. Just thinking about him makes me feel ill, yet he's never seemed more likable than in the last week or so."

Thinking back, I recall finding the man disagreeable, but thinking about him never made me feel ill. I nudge, "Try. Close your eyes and pretend you're reading the article that you want to write. What would it say?"

Andrew takes a deep breath and gulps some water after I force the tumbler into his hands.

The strain of the task at hand is evident on Andrew's brow. He closes his eyes and constructs his biography of the man who leads us to our destiny. "The wagon master, Joseph Roulette, is a bearded man of about forty, with bags under his eyes, and a worrisome-looking carbuncle on his neck. He is half French Canadian and half Lakota. After twenty years of working the fur trade, the trapper began leading emigrants to Oregon. We are instructed to refer to him as Boss Wheel. A pair of native scouts, Arikta and Dembi Koofai, and a man from Santa Fé, named Agapito Huerta Delgado, serve as the wagon master's crew. The tools of his trade include a long coat, called a capote, and he can often be seen sitting high in the saddle on a black horse named Clipper. Sometimes he gazes into a telescope. Other times, he squints at the horizon. When he feels everyone is safe, he smokes the foulest smelling tobacco. The cranky loner complains about greenhorns and delegates interpersonal dealings to his assistant, who he calls Pito rather than Agapito. Judging by his answers to interview questions, one surmises that when he is alone with his thoughts, the man thinks about his wife who lives in Chief Spotted Tail's Brulé Lakota village, or, maybe he relives in his mind his many annual sojourns to Rendezvous, the annual gathering of trappers, traders, and explorers. The man who has come to be known as Boss Wheel, on account of his last name, means *wheel* in French, has the gruff exterior of a fairytale billy goat and he might not want you to know it, but deep within his chest, there is a heart of gold."

Andrew takes a deep breath and is quiet for a moment. Then he asks, "Should I tell a couple of his old fashioned stories, Mama?"

"Yes, I think you should include his brother, and his friend, Jim Bridger, in the article as well. When we're settled in Oregon, let's mail it to the newspapers in New York." I ask Andrew if he's feeling any better, and he claims that he's feeling worse, not better.

"You know how a sick feeling takes me over before something bad happens, Mama?"

He does not need to remind me. I nod and grumble, "You've mentioned it." Of course, it must be superstition, but it is hard not to be fearful, nevertheless. That's how superstitions become powerful.

For a moment, Andrew sounds like an old man. He says, "It took me a long time to understand how it worked. I wish I knew what was going to happen so that I could stop it. Sometimes, I see flashes of things in my head, like when Father, Ellen, and Carter drank the water that killed them. I've been seeing those flashes again, Mama, only I can't make out many details."

I recall Rose telling me about her guardian angel's warning, and shiver. To a sensible adult, Rose and Andrew's concerns sound like a whole lot of nonsense. It takes some doing and it is increasingly challenging to convince myself that it's not all just coincidental. I've learned to be careful with my words, having offended Rose and driven a wedge between us. To Andrew I say, "Let me know if there's anything I can do to help." I escort him to the tent so that he can lie down.

SUNDAY, SEPTEMBER 1

LAST NIGHT, CHRISTOPHER SLEPT under Alvah's wagon. He wasn't eager to spend the night in the tent with Andrew, as ill as his brother claims to be. Since Andrew isn't feeling any better, I insist that he let Hollis examine him. The doctor doesn't have any better idea of what's wrong with Andrew than me, but his advice is the same. Fortunately for Andrew, today is a day off and I hope that he'll be feeling better by the time the wagon train departs tomorrow.

As I'm scrubbing laundry against the washboard, Christopher mopes into camp. "Remember that puppy I let you hold, Mama? The one that looked the most like Honey?"

I drop wet trousers onto the pan, dry my hands on my apron, and stand. "Yes, dear."

Christopher grips his broken arm with his good hand and looks at his forearm. "She died."

I'm sad for Christopher and I'm sure he can see that from my expression.

He speaks mournfully. "She seemed the healthiest of all of the puppies. We can't explain it, but she didn't make it. Now there are only two puppies left, Mama."

"Aw, I'm so sorry, Christopher."

I hold my arms wide to offer him comfort, but he just stands his ground. The boy isn't even ten. He may be able to block his tears, but he is not too old for the comfort of his Mama's arms. I step forward, drop to my knees, and wrap my arms around him. "I am so sorry, dear."

When I release him, he says, "Thanks Mama. I just thought you should know." He turns around and shuffles back across the circle to Alvah's camp.

As I return to the washboard, I blink back the tears that Christopher should have shed. I wonder if the dead puppy is the bad news that Andrew sensed was on the way.

When the wash and baking are done, boredom overtakes me. I check on Andrew, visit with Gwibunzi and the red, roan mare, and then I pick up my lasso. As a kid, I spent a lot of time throwing a rope. I got lucky when I roped Gwibunzi, and the roan let me drop the loop over her head. What if I had to throw a rope from afar? With my rope in hand, I step into the circle within the wagons. At a pace of ten steps from The Hub, I swing my loop and throw it over the post and tug gently, as if I were roping a steer.

Then, I pace back fifteen steps instead of ten. My loop soars through the air and drops over the wooden pillar, just as it did before.

On my next try, I step twenty paces away in a different direction and throw my rope again. Another ringer. Behind me, a couple of men cheer. I turn and see Agapito and the scouts, Arikta and Dembi Koofai. Boss Wheel must be watching over the encampment from a comfortable distance.

I step forward to The Hub, retrieve my loop, and measure a distance of twenty-five steps before trying again. This time, I miss and my audience groans. It isn't just the wagon master's camp. A crowd begins to gather. I step toward them. "Would anybody else like to try?"

Arikta volunteers. I hand him my lasso and Dembi Koofai follows Arikta. I step beneath the canvas awning beside the wagon master's camp.

Dahlia Jane toddles over from our wagon, and Agapito sweeps her into his arms. He plants a blizzard of smooches on her cheek. Then, he says, "How is it with you today, *amorcita?*"

She shrugs, touches his nose with her finger, and then giggles. Agapito kisses the tip of her nose and then sets her on the ground. A moment later, she trots back to the doll she left beneath our wagon.

We watch as men take turns roping the post and Agapito says, "It will not be long now. Soon, we will reach our destination. Do you think about Oregon a lot now?"

His question surprises me. "Not really. I think a lot about building a cabin. I can swing an axe, but I don't know anything about carpentry or building structures. I guess we'll have to rely on Stillman. He built our wagon, but then, maybe it's not the same thing as building a home. Other than that, I don't really think about Oregon. It's hard to see beyond the ruts in the trail."

"What about love, *estimada?* Do you ever think about that?"

I point at Sully, the older man that The Committee wanted me to marry when Larkin died. He sits, shirtless in front of his wagon, enjoying an idle moment. "I thought about it when I walked past Sully on my way to rope a post." I laugh and whisper to Agapito, "No. Thank you just the same."

Agapito chides, "*El amor*. It is a serious subject. It is not something to laugh about."

I put a hand over my heart and shake my head. "Oh, Agapito. I'm too old for such nonsense." I can't help stealing a glance into the man's face. "Sometimes, I like to imagine I'm not too old, and I'll admit my thoughts aren't always chaste, but love is for young people."

"What about Miranda Knox?" he challenges.

I fully understand the point he's making, but I pretend otherwise. "Miranda? Miranda Knox? I think she's too old for you, Agapito," I say, playfully.

He chuckles and waves off the notion with his hands. "No. You have not noticed? It looks to me like Sully and Miranda have found *el amor*. They are far older than you are."

The grin on Agapito's face compliments the spoken words that challenge my argument. I am not prepared to concede the point. Love, most definitely, is for young people. "Perhaps it is the curse of the Snake River that is to blame. You've heard Boss Wheel. Everybody has gone loco. How else could you explain Sully and Miranda?"

"*La serpiente*, you think she is to blame? I am not so sure, but *el amor* has been responsible for making lovers go loco."

I sigh. "To be young, in love, and crazy once again. Wouldn't that be something?"

"Yes. It is something to ponder, no?"

MONDAY, SEPTEMBER 2

AFTER A SHORT DAY, we make our way to the arid prominence known as Bonneville Point. When the wagons have circled, I venture off to find a private spot. On my way back to the wagons, a colorful flutter in a wild shrub catches my eye.

I crouch beside the tangled bitterbrush and unwind a neckerchief from the scraggy branches. The fabric is a little faded, but the cheerful tartan pattern remains. I turn the square of dark blue and forest green cloth in my hands and see the words, "The Radish" neatly stitched in white thread in a corner. What a curious thing to find.

When I return to camp, I show Andrew the Scottish bandanna. He holds it in his hand and his face bunches up. He frowns, shakes his head, and smacks his forehead a few times. "Get rid of it, Mama."

"Why?"

"I don't know. Ow, my stomach." He looks about nervously. "There's a taint to it. I can't explain it. What if it covered a bandit's face, Mama?"

"Nonsense, dear. It's just a piece of cloth. And look, somebody sewed the name of a vegetable into it." Why would they do such a thing? Radishes are crunchy and have a unique flavor, though many people prefer to avoid them. "Even if it belonged to a bandit, he's obviously long gone."

Andrew passes it back to me without looking at the stitches. "It's horrible, Mama. Get rid of it."

He isn't usually bossy with me. With his brother, maybe sometimes, but I'm not used to having him tell me what to do. Why should I discard such a useful object? I fold it and push it into my dress pocket. It will come in handy the next time somebody catches a cold or if there is another dust storm.

"I thought you were feeling better, dear." He didn't have any trouble keeping up with the oxen today and he only rode in the back of the wagon briefly while he was writing today's paper. "But you don't look too good now."

"It comes and goes, Mama. One minute, I feel normal. Then, suddenly, my mind races and I feel like a locomotive is crashing through my belly. Next thing I know it, bad things happen in my head. It's just..." Andrew bites his lip as if trying to figure out how to complete his thought... "hard to take."

"Maybe you should go back to the wagon and rest again."

"No, you see, Mama? Now I feel better again." He tells me not to worry about him and wanders away.

I stand for a moment, remove my hat, and let the breeze stir my hair. There's not a cloud in the enormous sky. The vast golden range that surrounds me looks beautiful now, whereas the exact same vista looked bleak the last several days. Maybe the hint of green in the distant river basin and the nearness of inviting mountains make the landscape seem more welcoming.

It's nice to welcome the sun and let it warm my cheeks. To avoid sunburns, I'm almost always sheltered beneath the wide brimmed hat which now feels like it belongs on my head. The gentle, late summer breeze is perfectly temperate. I should be glad that we've passed the sweltering heat of summer, and yet, that only means that the dangers of winter finding us before we reach the coast have increased.

I flip my hair, letting the breeze toss my mane. Just when I think that I've succeeded in banishing thoughts of love from my mind, the eternal temptation returns to torment me once again. I whisper Noah's name into the wind and refuse to allow the boy who melted my heart so long ago, back into my thoughts. I say Larkin's name, and add *Rest in peace, my friend*. He was my husband, best friend, and father to my children, but now he is gone. Lucky Nye's name springs from my lips. A good friend and middle aged fascination, yes, but we could never have found *el amor*, as Agapito puts it.

If it weren't for *that* man, I think I would be able to completely avoid irrational and torrid thoughts altogether. For the thousandth time, I list in my head all the reasons that Agapito and I could never marry. It's such a long list, I have to wonder, why do I even need to recite it to myself? There isn't the slightest reason to give it a moment's thought, until he's standing beside me. My resolve is far stronger when he isn't near.

I picture myself standing on top of Independence Rock, near the Sweetwater River, and smile. Ever since that day, I enjoy reliving that moment in my mind and the notion of feeling powerful inflates my resolve. I remind myself of my pledge to remain a woman alone.

The tempting smell of the man in the next wagon all too often swirls in my senses, quickens my pulse, and threatens to knock me from my perch. I shake myself and drop the hat back on my head. Why is the mere thought of that man so beguiling? The Devil himself could not choose a more captivating trickster to send my way, if he wanted to steal my soul. I curse myself. I've spent far too many Sunday mornings listening to Reverend Meadows. When it comes down to it, he doesn't make any more sense than Rose does when she whispers about ghosts, or now, Andrew's brooding, superstitious warnings.

Just because Agapito brought up the subject of love doesn't mean that he was propositioning me. It's not uncommon for people who care about one another to talk about such subjects, I'm sure.

A couple of young men are practicing the sport of archery, flinging arrows from a bow into a tree near the top of the hill. Lately, we've been reminded of the need to be ready to defend ourselves. I shall ask if I can join them.

TUESDAY, SEPTEMBER 3

AFTER A LONG DAY of travel, we reach the fertile valley I spied from Bonneville Point. We settle into a pleasant camp near the banks of the Boise River.

The water barrel isn't far from empty and will require many trips to replenish. On my second journey to the river, I encounter Hannah Knox. The older sister traveling with Rose's teenaged friend, Garland Knox, has neatly pinned, salt and peppered hair, and despite the rigors of travel, she looks like she never left home. Like her sister, Hannah dresses more formally than most travelers do. Some people's everyday clothes are other people's Sunday best. Perhaps back home, the sisters had servants to take care of them, but along The Oregon Trail, everyone must do their part.

We've been traveling together for months. I've spoken to everybody at one point or another. It's hard to recall having exchanged anything but pleasantries with this woman from Hillsborough, North Carolina.

As she dips a bucket into the river, I offer, "Good day, Miss Knox."

The frown on the woman's face doesn't match the politeness of her curt greeting. "How do you do?" She begins to step back toward the encampment, then stops and sets her water buckets on the ground.

"Is there something the matter, Miss Knox?"

It is as if the woman has forgotten my presence. She stands with a hand on her hip and points toward camp with a dismissive wave of a hand as Sully and Miranda stroll by, her sister's arm grasping the widower's elbow. Agapito was right about them. I think of the disagreeable man that offered to marry me after Larkin died and wonder what Miranda sees in him.

Hannah's sharp words are spoken crisply. "Imagine, a grown woman behaving like a lovesick chickadee."

It crosses my mind that Hannah's demeanor prepared Miranda for Sully. I think of the years Larkin and I spent bickering with one another. Why do people so often gravitate toward disagreeable people? I tell Miss Knox, "There's no explaining how the heart fancies what it does."

The woman looks at me like she didn't expect me to say anything in response to her rhetoric. "We're going to open a store in Oregon. I'll not have a man as a partner in the business. Miranda and I planned to run the shop together." She rubs her chin and I imagine that she's envisioning Sully intervening in the operation of her establishment.

"Are you planning to open a mercantile?"

Hannah turns toward me, facing me directly rather than having her shoulder pointed at me. Her right hand fondles a pendant with a bright emerald gemstone. "Heavens, no." There is excitement in her voice and her eyes glimmer as she talks about a store, just for ladies, full of dresses, jewelry, and the sort of things that appeal to city women. Not the utilitarian wares for the kitchen or larder. The way Hannah chatters about her vision for the shoppe makes me feel like I am her best acquaintance or a potential customer. It just goes to show that even people who always seem grouchy have something in them that makes their hearts sing. They say there's good in everyone and though I don't care much about dresses or jewelry, Hannah's unexpected enthusiasm is infectious.

Walking away with full buckets of water, I can't help rooting for both women. Love may be for young people, but somehow, it never called for Miranda until she was over fifty. Why not? Maybe Hannah will be better off on her own. That way, she can set up her emporium just as she wishes without having to compromise her vision with her sister's.

The question Agapito posed in Missouri niggles its way to the front of my mind again, "What is *your* dream? Not what is Larkin's dream. What is your dream?"

The Viper stares at the space between his brothers and begins to speak in a quiet but intense voice. "Pack up. It's time to hit the trail. We'll be gone for a few days at least. Our target draws closer." His piercing eyes seem capable of igniting fire from a borehole in the floorboards.

The Radish groans.

"It won't be long, kid. You'll have more painted ladies than you can handle. An assortment of women for your constant amusement." The Viper laughs

and imagines his kid brother begging to get away from it all. Surely, too much of such companionship will change the kid's mind about women. He'll see. "Keep your guns loaded and your powder dry."

The Viper turns his back to his brothers and raises his voice, speaking through the cabin's open door. "Soon the season will be over. Time is running out. The last of this year's wagons are coming along now. We've got enough money now to live 'the good life' for a couple of years, but not enough to last us forever. Forever is a long time. Forever is expensive. We'll never have as easy pickings as we got right now. It is time to make the most of it while we still can."

Sloan grumbles. "I'd give up on forever for a single day off."

The Viper turns and speaks in a menacing tone. "You don't mean that."

"Yes, I do."

"One more month, Sloan. Just one more month. After that, you'll never need to leave your room. If you want to, you can spend all day in bed, whenever y ou want."

The Viper steps into the doorway, forearms resting on the frame. "The big one is coming and it won't be long. It's time for us to ride out and meet it. We'll kill every man, woman, and child. We'll take every dollar they have. Instead of stealing a few horses, we'll take every miserable beast, down to the last ox and mule. We'll pick that wagon train clean and we'll be rich." The Viper's defiant stance relaxes. He turns and faces away from the cabin's interior. His chin lowers toward his chest and his gaze meets the dusty ground beyond the porch. "All our dreams will come true."

The Viper sounds sad as his last sentence rolls off his tongue. To himself he mutters, "All your dreams will come true."

WEDNESDAY, SEPTEMBER 4

AFTER ANOTHER LONG DAY of travel, we drop anchor near an enormous island that splits the river in two. As we complete the mundane tasks that accompany our daily arrivals, Snarling Wolf appears beside our crackling campfire. I cast a gaze about and see Rose climbing into the back of the wagon.

Without expression, my son-in-law says, "You asked us to tell you before we leave."

I drop my skillet. My hands spring to my cheeks. "Good Heavens." I want to argue and tell him all the reasons they should not go now, but they didn't have to tell me. Instead, they honored my wish. I know I should thank him for telling me and prepare to wish them well, but those words don't come to me. I lower myself to a box beside the fire and speak to the flames rather than my daughter's husband. "How long before you go?"

"We will go no farther than the end of the Snake."

We know that a new phase of the journey begins when we last see the Snake and that junction comes after a place called Farewell Bend. After that, we're told that the threat of outlaws attacking diminishes, but we must face steep and mountainous terrain after having traversed more level ground for so long. Some say the last several hundred miles are the most difficult, but that is inconceivable. It's hard to be impressed by the irony of parting with my firstborn child at a place called Farewell Bend. I was so afraid of this outcome, it is almost as if I willed it to happen. I rub my eyes. What can I do? The decision is not mine to make. In fact, it has already been decided. I stand and look into the man's eyes. "When do we reach the end? How much farther? How long do we have, Song Manitu Tanka Glow?"

"Ten days. At the rate we travel, it will be about ten days."

Rose has retrieved her eye paint from the back of the wagon. She walks purposefully toward us, slips her hand into Snarling Wolf's, and looks up into his face.

He says, "It has been told."

Rose nods and squints at me, lifting her upper lip, and looks like she might appear when staring into a blinding sun. Then the couple turns to leave.

An hour later, I wander away from the wagons and make my way toward their camp. Rose sits cross-legged beside a small campfire, her hands locked onto her knees, her eyelids freshly painted.

Snarling Wolf sits beside her, only his eyes are open. When I look at him, he climbs to his feet and reaches my side in a few quick strides. "Let us walk." He extends a hand, indicating a path along the river.

I nod and take a few slow steps. How do I voice my concerns?

"You wish to talk to me."

"I do."

"But you do not know what to say."

"How did you know?"

"I hear your thoughts."

As we stroll, I turn my head and give him a questioning look. Is he also mad? Perhaps I heard him incorrectly. "What did you just say?"

"I hear your thoughts. Not just you. Everybody. It has always been so."

I can feel my eyes blink rapidly.

"Now you are trying to think of something nice to say. You do not believe that I can read your thoughts. You do not believe Rose either. At least you believe that she *thinks* she speaks to the dead, even if you do not think that ghosts are real."

My head hangs low. I've tried to pretend that I understand her, but Song Manitu Tanka Glow knows better. The perceptive man must have seen a look on my face. Whatever clues I may have left about my disbelief, he has picked up on them, but that doesn't mean that he can hear my thoughts. Why doesn't he just run off into the woods and howl at the stars?

"I am not going to run off and leave Rose."

"I didn't say that you would."

"I do not howl at the stars."

My throat is dry when I swallow. It is uncanny. I don't believe in such nonsense, yet the man who claims to know what's on people's minds just spoke my thought, just as I phrased it in my head.

"Still, you doubt, yet I have proven it is so."

My feet stop and I pivot toward the man and he stands confidently facing me.

"You think I make lucky guesses." A couple of moments pass and my thoughts turn. "You are afraid because your daughter is young and Spotted Tail's village is far from Oregon."

I nod.

"Most people do not like Indians. You are different. You hate my name, that's why you try to say it in Lakota rather than English. But you do not hate me. You think I am loco, and you think Rose is loco, too. You pray for a miracle to keep your daughter with you. You understand that she is first a wife and then a daughter now, but you worry that she is too young. Most people do not think white girls should marry Indian men, but you are different. Now you are thinking about a young Indian you loved when you were her age. You wish that you could stop but you cannot. You grieve for him though he is not dead. You're mad at yourself for thinking of this man named Noah and you wish that I would stop speaking your thoughts out loud. You still do not want to believe, yet I have followed the twisting trail of your thoughts. Now you are thinking that it is not fair to read people's private thoughts, therefore you must have started to believe a little bit. I could not have guessed these things, Dorcas."

"You say you can read everybody's thoughts, not just mine. I've never imagined such a thing. Can you read the outlaws' thoughts? These bandits that everybody fears, can you conjure up their minds?"

"I can only read the thoughts of people when they are nearby. The closer they are, the stronger the message. Now you are thinking about whether you can think a lie, would I believe it? It doesn't work that way. You would be surprised how often people lie. I am used to it and do not judge anymore. Most people lie more than you do, Dorcas. Mostly, you just lie to yourself."

"Is there anybody whose thoughts you cannot invade?"

"Yes. Most of the time, I cannot read Rose's thoughts. That is because most of her thoughts occur in the spirit world rather than ours."

I take a step backward, my right foot trips, and I stumble. Snarling Wolf steps forward and steadies me before I crash to the ground.

When I'm back on firm ground, Snarling Wolf says, "You still want to find a way to resist the truths I have spoken. You tell yourself that you will think about it later. You do not want time to understand better. You think if you can get away from your thoughts, you can make them go away, but these miracles surround you. Whenever you begin to understand them, you quickly blink your thoughts away so that you can deny them. You wish that you could blink your mind blank so that I will stop, but it does not work that way. Very few people can control their own thoughts."

He stares at me blankly as if his own mind were as empty as the endless desert that surrounds us. I've had enough and have grown weary of this conversation.

"That is not very nice, Dorcas."

"What?"

"You wish that I would choke on a bone. You are picturing me as a wolf again."

I stomp my foot and storm away.

The Viper and his brothers lie on their bellies, looking at the gathered wagons from a distant hilltop. The oldest brother hisses, "Why must they move so s lowly?"

Sloan says, "Why don't we just take 'em now? Let's get it over with."

"No," The Viper snaps. "Not until we have them where we want them. We must stick to the plan."

The Radish's belly grumbles so loudly that his brothers can hear it and the splayed bandits crawl backward through the dust like half-crazed spiders.

Thursday, September 5

In the middle of the night, I wake up sweaty and screaming. Dahlia Jane is on her knees, screaming back at me. I blink rapidly, trying to flip away a gruesome nightmare.

Time slows and I picture Rose striding through Spotted Tail's village, her pregnant belly expanding as if each second were a day until she howls in pain and struggles to deliver a child. Instead of a baby, Rose delivers a massive litter of wolf whelps. A shiver blows across my arm and I swallow three times. More than a dozen reddish brown wiggling curs with straggly, irregular fur fight over the chance to nurse at Rose's barren bosom. Why can't I shake off the image?

I pull Dahlia Jane into a hug and shush her. Just as I get the child back to sleep, the trumpet blasts. Another day of marching is upon us. Memories of last night's dream battle in my thoughts with recollections of yesterday's conversation with Snarling Wolf. Everything he said seems so outlandish, yet sentence after spoken sentence, he put my thoughts to words. Trying to deny it is like disowning a long shadow on a sunny afternoon.

When the wagons circle for the evening, Snarling Wolf steps into camp and drops a plump sage hen beside the fire. After thanking him for bringing us fresh meat, I whisper, "I want to believe you, Snarling Wolf."

"No, you don't."

I stand back, startled. How dare he accuse me of lying. Good Heavens, he's right. I don't want to believe him at all, but I struggle to admit to myself just what I do want. Finally, I find the words to say, "Very well. How about this: I want to try to believe."

"That sounds closer to the truth. You're thinking about when I told you that miracles surround you." My busy family scurries around doing all too familiar chores.

I'm sure I must be scowling when I say, "Yes. I haven't thought about much else."

The man frowns as if seeing the dream I had last night. He thrusts a shoulder toward my youngest son, as if pointing toward him with a finger. He says, "Look at Christopher. He brings the chickens fresh greens. He feels their hunger and tends their needs. Think back, Dorcas. He has always been like this, hasn't he? He is like you. You have a deep sympathy for animals and could be like Christopher, if you let yourself. He is not just compassionate. He feels what they do. There is a difference."

I nod. It is hard to deny. Christopher has always shared a special bond with animals. It is strongest with dogs. I picture a growling beast with dagger-sized incisors, and shudder. Snarling Wolf ignores my thought.

"Look at Andrew. He glances at the sky and can read the clouds, but it is more than that. He often knows what will happen before it does. Usually, he sees glimpses but not the whole thing, and he cannot tell when he is seeing something that will happen a long time from now or very soon. He is often confused and this causes him pain. It is a frightening burden, yet he bears it well. You have noticed this. Am I wrong?"

For some reason, I find it easier to accept Andrew's predictions than the other bizarre notions that Snarling Wolf suggests. Maybe after having been one hundred percent correct about the weather for so long that I don't even think of the skill as uncommon makes it seem less cosmic than reading thoughts or sensing animals' feelings.

"And Rose. She does not make a lot of sense in *your* world. She often cannot remember what happens in the world of spirits when she shifts back and forth, but sometimes she does remember. When her thoughts are on this side of the veil and her memories travel back with her, I can read her mind then. So many people need help finding their way to the world of spirits. Too many become trapped where they don't belong and this causes Rose pain. It is too bad there aren't more people like your daughter. She has an uncommon gift, Dorcas, and she helps people in ways that other people cannot. That's what I mean when I say, these miracles surround you."

I shift my weight from one leg to another.

"And your youngest child shares your nightmares. When you sleep, she sees your dreams the same as you do."

My hands cover my face. The poor child. I recall my horrible dream from last night and desperately beg Snarling Wolf. "You must stop. You're scaring me. I don't want to hear anything more about it."

Snarling Wolf tips his head forward and looks at me harshly. "One day you will trust and understand."

It gets my hackles up. Is he being harsh and critical? Is he making a prediction or stating what he believes to be a fact? It sounds like a threat to me.

From a thick stand of cottonwoods on the other side of the river, The Viper and his brothers watch over the camp, studying its inhabitants. Sloan and the Radish sit at the base of a tree, leaning against a stump. The Viper lies on his belly, ten feet away. "Have you noticed that Indian traveling alongside the wagons? He camps with a white woman, a short distance away. She looks more like a girl than a woman."

Sloan shrugs. "So what?"

The Viper ignores his brother. "And the scouts are Indians, also. We have seen this crew before. We must be wary."

The Radish says, "Can we even the odds?"

Sloan adds, "Anything we can do to make the job easier?"

The Viper grunts. Maybe there is hope for his brothers yet. A big job like this requires a high level of tactical planning and at the same time, wily bandits must always be flexible enough to modify plans when adjustments need to be made. The watchful wagon boss and his diligent scouts are to be expected. This unpredictable, roving Indian on the fringes is an added worry.

FRIDAY, SEPTEMBER 6

ALL MORNING, THE LAST couple of wagons lag. Just before the mid-day break, I step back to ask if I can help. The last wagon belongs to the strapping Butler Grimes, and the second to last wagon is driven by the teenager, Garland Knox.

"What's wrong, Gar?"

The fourteen-year-old tips his head back and peers up at me from under his hat. "I can't goad 'em any faster, ma'am. It's all I can do to move them at all. It's as if they plumb wore out."

I think back to when I forced our kine to haul Larkin's safe and remember Agapito constantly telling us to lighten the load. Now, four oxen pull our wagon well enough. Six oxen should do fine with the Knox wagon. I wonder if Hannah is carrying stock for the store she plans to open in Oregon. Perhaps she can ask Sully to haul some of their belongings. How much could he be carrying in his wagon?

Everything appears fine in the Grimes wagon. The family of four is seated on a bench in the front of the wagon and the team of mules doesn't seem to have any difficulty keeping up with Garland and his aunts. I think back to the time when the Grimes' mules crashed into the back of the Knox's wagon. It's hard to recall how long ago that was. It seems like years since that happened. Boss Wheel griped about the greenhorns and an image of heavy chests in the Knox wagons returns to my mind.

Either at noon or at the end of the day, I shall suggest that some of their load be shifted to another wagon. I'm surprised that the wagon master hasn't ordered them to cast off their excesses.

Just ahead, the Franklin's wagon disappears around a bend in the trail ahead, leaving us isolated from the rest of the procession.

"Do you have another bullwhip, Gar? Maybe if we push from both sides they'll step faster."

"Naw. Sorry, ma'am. I don't."

"Let me take a turn. Maybe a different voice will jostle them from their doldrums."

As I snap the whip and scream my loudest, I think back to when we left Independence, Missouri, and I was disinclined to whip the oxen. How many months ago was that now?

I glance back at the Grimes wagon behind us and I'm stunned to see four horsemen galloping toward the Grimes wagon from the direction of the river. I scream to warn them, shove the bullwhip back at Garland, and run toward the Grimes wagon while pointing at the riders, but I'm too late.

The mules have halted and four curly haired men with bandana-covered faces have the Grimes family surrounded. The highwaymen wear matching clothes and look like brothers. Even the guns they have drawn look identical.

Three revolvers are pointed at the young family and one man points his weapon at me.

I shout, "What do you think you're doing?"

"Shut up, lady, or I'll blow a hole in ya."

Another bandit shouts at Butler Grimes. Grimes stands, pulls his pockets inside out, and says, "We're broke. We spent our last dollar."

"You're lying. Hand over your stake or we'll ransack your wagon. We'll trade your babies to the Injuns."

Betty squeezes four-year-old Lulu so hard, the toddler begins to cry.

Butler's voice raises. "We got nothing. I swear."

Betty yells. "I got some money, mister. My pa gave me some. I never told him. You can have it, just leave us alone."

"Get it fast. No funny business. How much you got?"

"Thirty dollars. It's in the back."

One of the highwaymen rides around to the back and watches Betty as she climbs into the wagon and pulls a small, drawstring bag from a box in the wagon.

As Betty emerges from the wagon, the man that threatened to sell the Grimes children says, "Throw that down here. Now."

The man whose gun points at me signals to the others. Our absence has been noticed. Boss Wheel and the scouts gallop toward us.

With a double grunt, the outlaws kick their horses and gallop off along the trail toward the southeast.

The matching, dark brown horses with black tails are fast. Butler tries to reassure his family as Betty retreats with their son and daughter beneath the cover of their wagon.

Boss Wheel says, "What happened, greenhorn?"

The yammering man trips over his tongue, and I answer Boss Wheel's question. "They've been robbed. Those four riders made off with a sack of money."

"How much did they get?"

Butler manages to squeak out, "Don't rightly know. I thought we was broke. Seems like Betty's daddy gave her a stash."

"I'm sorry I didn't tell you. Pa told me not to tell anyone. It was thirty dollars."

"Gosh. Thirty bucks! Now we're really busted."

Butler's six-year-old towhead, Dean, repeats, "Gosh. Thirty bucks."

The wagon boss tells Arikta to stay with the Grimes family, then says to me, "What are you doing here, anyway?"

When I tell him that I came back to see what was holding up the last two wagons, Boss Wheel grunts approvingly.

At dinner, Andrew interviews Butler and Betty as well as Garland and his aunts who shivered in fear in the back of their wagon during the stick up. In a special editorial, Andrew warns of the many perils ahead. "Lest we be lulled into complacency by the thought that we've already seen the ire of a parade of marauding elephants, we must expect more danger ahead."

Hannah is spooked about riding last in line tomorrow with six oxen that can't keep up. The sanctimonious woman quickly sees the merit to my whispered suggestion and sends Miranda to ask her beau if he could take on some of their weight.

Andrew grumbles when I volunteer him to help Garland lug cartons, crates, satchels, and chests to Sully's wagon.

The Hub buzzes with concerned travelers. Some share Andrew's concern that there is more thievery in our future whereas others think now that we've been robbed, the path ahead is safer.

Reverend Meadows passes around a hat. "The Grimes are penniless. The thugs took their very last cent."

It's easy to be generous when you have money to spare, but we're down to our last twenty dollars. I frown when Reverend Meadows counts the funds in the hat, and Butler thanks everyone for their generosity. I don't begrudge their fifteen dollars, though they have more than we do. I wonder how much money we have left, all of us combined.

At dusk, Sloan tells his brothers about the hold up. "Four gunmen robbed the last wagon just before the mid-day break. They were solid built, not skinny, like us. They're well dressed, have fancy matching horses, and I don't know if they got away with anything or not. They didn't have the stragglers covered yesterday. Bet they will tomorrow. Maybe we can take advantage and hit the front end."

The Viper's eyes dart around in their sockets, as if sorting thoughts in his head, putting some facts in one spot and others in another. "No, the plan remains. We'll pick at them first, then wipe 'em out later."

The Radish gripes, "Those hoodlums got away with some of our take. We should go after them."

"No. We stick to the plan, confound it. How many times I gotta tell you?" The Viper unleashes a tirade of curse words upon his brothers.

SATURDAY, SEPTEMBER 7

AFTER AN EASY CROSSING of the Boise River and a modest travel day, the consensus is that our worst days are behind us. The coastal South Carolinians had borne the brunt of the outlaws' onslaught and now we can travel without worry.

As we set up camp along a pleasant bend in the river, the urge to congregate becomes unstoppable. Word of gathering for a dance travels up and down the line as families hurry to put away provisions. Bathers along the riverside freshen up, eager to wash away their troubles.

Meanwhile, Andrew issues warnings in the newspaper. Most people are too busy to read it and the few that do aren't in the mood to heed his editorial.

At the river, I find myself in the company of Addie and Esther. Addie can't stop talking and Esther has little to say to me. There's nothing I can say to convince Esther that I did not tell Rose, or anybody else about her dalliance with Armand Bartholomieux. Clearly, Addie and Esther have remained close. Neither woman seems to have made friends beyond one another.

Addie says to me, "You almost never come around anymore. It is like you have become one of the men rather than one of the women. I should think it is enough to do the work of a woman without also having to do men's work. Why, you've practically become another member of the wagon master's crew."

I put my old friend off with a dismissive sentiment. "We get by." Why should I always have to visit her? The woman barely leaves the side of her wagon. "You're welcome to stop by anytime you wish." I don't care whether she thinks I'm sufficiently ladylike. I'm content to wear a dress over my trousers, but I will no longer ride sidesaddle or wear a corset. It's been some time since anyone objected to the fact I wear Larkin's hat and tote his guns.

Fiddles beckon as we finish bathing and dress in fresh clothing. As the sun edges toward the horizon, the assistant wagon master jubilantly calls the celebratory sequence of moves. Enthusiastic dancers spiral in floral patterns. The festive sounds of laughter and amusement join the wail of strings and the beat of drums. The popping sound of gunfire goes unheard. Sitting at the edge of the crowd, I barely hear it myself, distracted by my thoughts and think nothing of it until I see Dembi Koofai slink through the crowd and whisper into Agapito's ear.

The assistant wagon master tells the carpenter, Schuyler Steele, to take over and follows the Shoshone scout. Now worried, I trail them as they make their way beyond our camp to the place where Snarling Wolf and Rose set up their tent.

My son-in-law has been shot. The bullet blew a gaping hole through the man's muscular chest and his dead body lies crumpled in a heap on the ground. His legs and arms are akimbo, like a hastily dropped stack of kindling. His head is snapped back, exposing his thick neck, and his long, black hair flutters in the evening breeze. I cross my arms and clutch my elbows. "Who could do such a thing?" I look about for my daughter. "Where's Rose?"

Not knowing what else to do, I hurry forward and stretch the corpse into a more dignified position. Agapito examines the wound, not bothering to confirm that the man is dead. Nobody could survive such a perfectly placed bullet. He speaks to the scout. "Where was the shooter? He could not have been far away."

Dembi Koofai points to a small cluster of gathered shrubs. It is as if someone set up a hunting blind for the purpose of firing the shot that killed Snarling Wolf. The murderer must have been just outside of the Lakota mind reader's radius. If only he could have read minds from farther away. I tip my head and spread my hand over my forehead. I feel guilty knowing that I had wished my son-in-law would disappear on numerous occasions. I never wished his death, but I feel complicit.

Agapito sends Dembi Koofai back to camp to get Arikta and a stretcher. Then he turns to me. "I am sorry, *estimada*. I wish you had not followed me. You should not have to see this."

I turn my head away and look back toward the circled wagons. "I must find Rose. Good Heavens, Agapito. What next?" Without waiting for an answer, I turn back to the man and say, "Do not bury him. Rose and Boss Wheel will know what to do." Where on earth did Rose go? Could she have returned to the wagon? Did she see what happened?

I run back to the wagon as fast as I've ever run anywhere. Though it is the first place I looked, I'm stunned to see Rose beneath our wagon where

Stillman ordinarily sleeps. Her legs are stretched out before her, and she is bent at the waist. She looks at her knees and talks to herself in a mumbling blather. I can't make out a word she says until she speaks to me. "You are not to blame, Mama. Song Manitu Tanka Glow says he should have listened to Andrew. He wants you to remember what he told you. In the spring, he wants me to go to live with Sees Through Clouds in Washakie's village."

Before I can acknowledge or object, Rose resumes her unintelligible chatter. She never even looked up at me. I try to imagine the black paint on her eyelids. Has she been crying? Is the paint smeared all over her face? Should I stay at her side? I know better than to interrupt her at such a time. I breathe life back into the wasting embers from our supper fire and listen to the distant music as I watch my daughter. I had barely become accustomed to having a married daughter and son-in-law, and now Rose and I have widowhood in common.

Andrew walks from the dance with his head drooping. "Agapito told me about Snarling Wolf. I knew something bad was going to happen. Why won't anybody listen to my warnings, Mama?"

Five miles away, The Viper waits for news. He doesn't turn to look at them when his brothers approach. "Well?"

The Radish says, "We got him."

"Who pulled the trigger?"

Sloan says, "I did. Blew a hole clean through his chest."

"Did his woman see it happen?"

"Dunno. I never saw her."

"She see you?"

"How should I know? I never saw her."

"Where was The Radish?"

The youngest outlaw says, "I stayed with the horses."

The Viper's grunt indicates satisfaction with his brothers' work.

Thank you for reading Snarling Wolf. You've made it across many rivers, but there are more crossings ahead of you.

Don't miss the heart-pounding climax of the Ghosts Along the Oregon Trail series. As the wagon train approaches the final leg of the journey, the looming threat of outlaws intensifies. The notorious bandit known as The Viper and his ruthless brothers are determined to rob the greenhorns, sell their stock, and kill every last one of them. What will become of Dorcas Moon, her family, and their friends? Will anyone survive the perilous journey? Rejoin the expedition and witness the thrilling end to a gripping saga.

Start reading *Rolling Home* today.

I hope to become one of your favorite new authors. Sign up for my email list at: https://www.itsoag.com/contact so you can stay up-to-date on upcoming releases, special offers, and exclusive giveaways. As a thank you, I'll send you a special Ghosts Along the Oregon Trail word search puzzle.

Jump Back In

Don't let the dust settle on your wagon!

Scan the QR code and leap to David Fitz-Gerald's website where you can find the links to the next installment in Ghosts Along the Oregon Trail.

ABOUT THE AUTHOR

DAVID FITZ-GERALD WRITES WESTERNS and historical fiction. He is the author of twelve books, including the brand-new series, Ghosts Along the Oregon Trail set in 1850. He's a multiple Laramie Award, first place, best in category winner; a Blue Ribbon Chanticleerian; a member of Western Writers of America; and a member of the Historical Novel Society.

Alpine landscapes and flashy horses always catch Dave's eye and turn his head. He is also an Adirondack 46-er, which means that he has hiked to the summit of the range's highest peaks. As a mountaineer, he's happiest at an elevation of over four thousand feet above sea level.

Dave is a lifelong fan of western fiction, landscapes, movies, and music. It should be no surprise that Dave delights in placing memorable characters on treacherous trails, mountain tops, and on the backs of wild horses.

Rejoin the expedition and witness the thrilling end to a gripping saga. Book 5 in the Ghosts Along the Oregon Trail series is *Rolling Home*!

A TIP OF THE HAT

This series is affectionately dedicated to the countless authors whose words have preserved the legend of the Oregon Trail, the diligent historians who have meticulously chronicled its history, and the brave emigrants who embarked on a perilous journey in pursuit of lofty dreams. Additionally, this series pays tribute to the indigenous peoples whose ancestors lived, loved, and died in these lands since ancient times. The rugged peaks and fruited plains, simultaneously abundant and inhospitable, bore witness to their stories. May their tales always echo through the canyons of history, preserving the spirit and honoring the legacy of those who walked the path before planes, trains, and automobiles.

Thank you to the collaborators that helped me bring Ghosts Along the Oregon Trail to life: editors Kolton Fitz-Gerald and Lindsay Fitzgerald; singer songwriter Kyle Hughes; White Rabbit Arts at the Historical Fiction Company; and the coaches at Author Ad School.

Deep gratitude to my Facebook group, Adirondack Spirit Guides. I appreciate the guidance, support, and early reader feedback. A special nod to Gail Cook, who was the first to make it through the series.

This project also pays homage to a genre that I've loved as long as I can remember. The old west in fiction, history books, landscape paintings, movies, television and songs inspired this project. If you think a character name is similar to an iconic western hero, you're not mistaken. Some of the characters' names were pulled from the roots of my family tree. For example, a woman named Dorcas is my 6th great-grandaunt. Many monikers are plucked from film credits. The unusual character, Fritz Franzwa is named to honor the work of a dedicated historian who researched, documented, and published *The Oregon Trail Revisited* and *Maps of the Oregon Trail*, which helped me cast my fictional emigrants on an incredible trail.

During my research for this project, I had the opportunity to visit many of the Oregon Trail's landmarks. It could take a lifetime to visit them all, but I'm well on my way. I've had the pleasure of crisscrossing the historic trail on the scenic byways in Wyoming and Nebraska, and I recall a sweltering day during a record-breaking heatwave in the 1980s. My brother, Jeff, and I visited the mostly abandoned town of Jeffrey City, Wyoming, which boasted a population of three. It's situated near the Oregon Trail and the Sweetwater River. We purchased soft drinks, but by the time we made it back to the truck, the red cans had already gone warm. It was *that* hot. The truck wasn't air conditioned, and I remember sympathizing with the pioneers, trudging along beside a chain of wagons. More recently, I had the pleasure of visiting the National Frontier Trails Museum in Independence, Missouri; the Fort Bridger State Historic Site; and the White Mountain Petroglyphs. It's off the trail, but I just had to send my characters there.

I'm *most* grateful to *you* for stepping away from the present, into the distant past with me. Thank you. I'd love to hear from you. If you get a chance to drop me an email at dave@itsoag.com, I'd love to know: if you were alive in 1850, would you have chosen to follow the Oregon Trail?

Made in United States
Troutdale, OR
11/24/2024

25138234R00147